'There's on
to prove t
interested ir

'What?' Lucy asked.

'Show him you're off-limits—you're someone else's girl. If he knows you're still single, he'll think you're pining for him. Whereas if he sees you with someone…he'll know you're not. And then he'll leave you alone.'

The volcano was about to explode at any minute, Nic thought.

Instead she nodded. 'Good point.'

She was going to go ahead with it?

'What's the plan?'

He didn't have one! 'We go back onto the ward. He overhears you make a date with the man in your life.' This was the crunch. The bit where she'd say no. 'Me.'

'And you think it'd work?'

Yes! Yes! his heart screamed. 'It's worth a try,' he said, as casually as he could.

Kate Hardy lives on the outskirts of Norwich with her husband, two small children, two lazy spaniels—and too many books to count! She wrote her first book at six, when her parents gave her a typewriter for her birthday. She had the first of a series of sexy romances published at age twenty-five, and swapped a job in marketing communications for freelance health journalism when her son was born so she could spend more time with him. She's wanted to write for Mills & Boon® since she was twelve—and when she was pregnant with her daughter, her husband pointed out that writing Medical Romances™ would be the perfect way to combine her interest in health issues with her love of good stories. It really is the best of both worlds—especially as she gets to meet a new gorgeous hero every time…

Recent titles by the same author:

THE ITALIAN DOCTOR'S PROPOSAL

BY
KATE HARDY

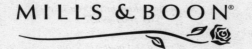

MILLS & BOON®

For Richard and Chrissy—
the best uncle and aunt in the world.

*First published in Great Britain 2003
Harlequin Mills & Boon Limited,
Eton House, 18-24 Paradise Road, Richmond, Surrey TW9 1SR*

© Pamela Brooks 2003

ISBN 0 263 83475 1

*Set in Times Roman 10½ on 12 pt.
03-1003-49557*

*Printed and bound in Spain
by Litografia Rosés, S.A., Barcelona*

PROLOGUE

'YOUR money or your life?'

Lucy whirled round and stared at the highwayman. She didn't recognise the voice or the lower half of his face not hidden by the domino mask. Or the dark hazel eyes, a curious mix of brown and grey that somehow managed to be soft and piercing at the same time.

Dangerous eyes.

Your money or your life?

Without giving her a chance to answer, he smiled at her. A smile that was even more dangerous than his eyes. A smile that started a small, slow smoulder in the pit of her stomach.

He was a walking definition of gorgeous. Dark hair that curled beneath a flat-crowned black hat; smooth olive skin; a loose white silk shirt, laced half-open to reveal a sprinkling of dark hair on his chest; tight black trousers leading down to highly polished black boots; and a silky black cloak.

Every woman's dream highwayman.

Including Lucy's.

'A kiss would do,' he said huskily, and leaned forward to claim it.

As kisses went, it was fairly chaste. And in the middle of a very public arena: the staff charity fancy-dress ball at Treverro Hospital. But the touch of his mouth against hers did something to her. Lucy's knees actually buckled. If he hadn't been supporting both her elbows, she would have fallen flat on her face.

5

And it got worse.

Because when he broke the kiss and pulled back just far enough to see her face, she saw it in his eyes. He *knew* what effect he'd had on her. He knew he'd blown just about every fuse in her body. And his eyes said that if she'd let him, he'd blow the ones she didn't even know she had.

'Catch you later, princess,' he said, then tipped his hat briefly, gave her a broad wink and spun on his heel as he wrapped his black cloak back round him.

It was completely theatrical and over the top. She should have laughed. Except she felt too sick when she realised what had just happened. Whoever the highwayman was, that kiss had been a set-up. A very public one. She could guess just who'd put him up to it, too—even what he'd said. 'Lucy's an ice maiden. It's about time someone proved she melts.'

She gritted her teeth. If she ever—*ever*—came across the highwayman again, she'd roast him alive.

And as for her SHO...Malcolm Hobart had better hope she was in a better mood when she was back on duty tomorrow morning.

CHAPTER ONE

'HARD luck, Luce.'

Lucy forced herself not to make the response that rose instantly to her lips—a snarl of 'don't call me Luce'—knowing that Mal just wanted to get a rise out of her. She wasn't going to give him the satisfaction of knowing he'd managed to rattle her. Though once she'd done the ward rounds, she was going to have a private word with him about practical jokes.

One practical joke in particular.

'You know, that job really should've been yours,' Mal continued.

'Obviously the powers that be thought differently.' She gave what she hoped looked like a philosophical shrug. 'Was there something specific you wanted to ask me about, Malcy, dearest, or can we do the ward round now?'

He whistled. 'You're really sore about it, aren't you? Losing out to Nic Alberici like that, when everyone thought the job had your name on it.'

'I am *not* sore,' Lucy said through gritted teeth.

'Lucy Williams, obstetric consultant. Sounds good.' Mal gave her a mischievous look. 'Maybe if you'd been *Luke* Williams, you'd have been in with a better chance.'

Lucy knew better than to listen to Mal—and better still than to let him wind her up. And far better than to say what he clearly believed she was thinking. So why did she have to open her mouth and say it? 'Jobs for the boys, isn't it, Mal? And as I'm not intending to have a sex change and

7

become an Italian playboy to suit the hospital bigwigs, I'll just have to lump it, won't I?'

Too late, she saw Rosemary, the senior midwife, shaking her head, grimacing and holding her hands up flat and crossed, moving them slightly but very fast: the age-old signal for 'stop right there'.

Too late, she heard a sultry voice behind her say, 'It's *half*-Italian, actually. My mother's English.'

Please, earth, open up and swallow me right now.

It didn't.

Please? she tried again.

Not even a tiny dent in the tiles, let alone the huge pit she needed.

So there was only one thing for it. Face her embarrassment head-on. She stopped holding her breath and spun round on her heel, ready to apologise to Nic Alberici for her rudeness and reassure him that she was looking forward to working with him...

And then she saw his eyes. Dark hazel eyes, a curious mixture of brown and grey. Eyes she'd seen before. Except this time they weren't warm and smiling and sexy and knowing. This time, they were cold and absolutely furious.

Can today get any worse? she thought. The man who'd embarrassed her at the fancy-dress ball was her new boss. So she couldn't bawl him out, the way she'd promised herself she would.

She also couldn't give in to the feelings that threatened to make her knees buckle again. He was her *boss*, for goodness' sake.

So there was only one thing she could do. Be professional.

She lifted her chin. 'I'm sorry. You must be Mr Alberici,' she said politely, extending her hand. 'Lucy Williams, special reg. Welcome to River Ward.'

He didn't take it. 'Jobs for the boys—an Italian play-boy, hmm?'

Uh-oh. Raw nerve. She shrugged. 'Figure of speech. It wasn't personal.'

'I think, Dr Williams—' his emphasis of her title made it clear he wasn't going to be easily mollified '—that you and I need a little chat. Sooner rather than later. Perhaps we could go to my office?'

She could see Mal's smirk out of the corner of her eye and could have kicked herself. But it was her own fault. She knew what Mal was like: he put everyone else out of the running for the wooden spoon award. He'd probably spotted Nic Alberici coming their way when he'd started needling her about the fact she hadn't got the consultant's post. She should have second-guessed Mal and avoided the subject. Now she and Nic Alberici had got off on the wrong foot. Just what she didn't need.

Meekly, she followed Nic to his office. The office *she'd* been using for the last month or so as acting consultant.

He gestured to her to sit down opposite him.

'I'm sorry you overheard that,' she said quietly.

'Clearly I wasn't meant to.' If anything, his eyes had grown even colder.

And she'd always thought brown eyes were warm. Lucy swallowed. 'I shouldn't have said it in the first place.'

'If you're going to have a problem working with me, Dr Williams, I'd prefer to be the first to know,' he said. 'It's important that patients—'

'Feel confident in the team working with them,' Lucy cut in. 'I agree. And I don't have a problem working with you, Mr Alberici. What you overheard...' She paused, wondering how to say it without making it sound as if she was blaming Mal, too gutless to take responsibility for her own mistakes. 'It's not the way *I* think. It's the way some of the other staff believe I think.'

'Ever heard the saying, "Perception is reality"?'

'Yes, but not in this case. I admit I thought I'd get the consultant's job; I've been standing in as acting consultant ever since Mike left. But you're older than I am, you're more experienced and you've a good reputation.' And he was better qualified. 'So you were the better candidate and I'm sure I can learn something from you.'

He didn't look convinced. 'So why…?'

'Why did I say that to Mal?' She shrugged. 'You know Mal.' Of course he did. Hadn't Mal been the one to talk him into kissing her at the charity ball? She ignored the tiny niggle of doubt, and continued, 'Work it out for yourself.'

There was a long, very awkward pause.

Finally, he spoke. 'So what now?'

'I apologise again, I reassure you that I'm a professional, you accept it—' Lucy ticked off the points on her fingers '—and we do the ward round before our pregnant mums get discharged with their three-day-old babies.'

His lips quirked at that. So he had a sense of humour. Well, that was a start.

'Apology accepted, Dr Williams.' The warmth she'd seen when he'd kissed her was slowly seeping back into his eyes. Not to mention the warmth in the pit of her stomach. Why did he have to have a smile like that? Why couldn't he have been…well, middle-aged and dull and not the slightest bit sexy?

Not to mention that voice. The slight accent that made her wonder what his voice would sound like in passion…

No. She was *not* going to start thinking like that about anyone, let alone her new boss. She was a professional. And she was completely focused on her career.

'Though I prefer to work on first-name terms,' he said. 'Call me Nic.'

The slight hint of a long 'i', a sensual Italian 'Nic' rather than a diffident English 'Nick'.

She had to get her libido back under control. Fast. Hadn't she already learned the hard way that it was stupid to follow her hormones instead of her head?

'Lucy.' She made it sound as cool and English as she could. Ice maiden. To match her reputation. She held her hand out. 'And I meant what I said. I'm looking forward to working with you.'

His handshake was firm and cool and professional. So why was her blood fizzing where he'd touched her? And if a handshake did this to her, what would a more intimate…? No. She forced the thought to the back of her mind. 'Shall we?'

He nodded and they went to join Rosemary and Mal. Just as Rosemary was about to update them on the first patient, Lucy's bleeper went.

'Sorry,' she mouthed, headed for the phone and dialled the number on her bleeper.

'Lucy Williams—you paged me?'

'Thanks for ringing back,' the A and E nurse said. 'We have a patient with a suspected placental abruption.' Placental abruption was where part of the placenta became detached from the uterus. It could be dangerous, possibly even fatal to both the mother and the baby. If the bleeding was severe, they'd need to do an emergency delivery.

'Have you done an ultrasound?' Lucy asked.

'A machine's on its way. Could you take a look at her?' the nurse asked.

'I'll be right down.' Though it was only courtesy to let her new boss know where she was going. She hated interrupting colleagues when they were with patients, but the only other choice was leaving a message with one of the midwives, and he'd probably think she was sulking and using any excuse to avoid him. She pulled back the curtain just enough to put her head through the gap. 'Mr Alberici, I'm sorry to interrupt. Could I have a quick word, please?'

'Of course. Please, excuse me,' he said to the patient, then came to join Lucy in the middle of the ward. 'What's up?'

'We've got a patient with a suspected placental abruption in A and E. They've asked me to see her.'

'I'll come with you—if it *is* that, we'll need her in Theatre pronto. You'll assist?'

Yeah, he *would* be a qualified obstetric surgeon. He could have offered to assist *her*. But, no, he had to take charge. 'Sure,' she muttered.

'I'll brief Mal and I'll be right with you,' he said.

Efficient, courteous—to the patients, if not to her—and drop-dead gorgeous. It was a tempting combination. A dangerous combination.

Stop it, she warned herself. You are *not* going to think about Nic Alberici like that.

Though in her mind's eye he wasn't wearing a formal white silk shirt, teamed with a silk tie and an expensively cut dark grey suit and topped with a white coat. He was wearing that half-open white shirt, tight black trousers, a hat and a domino mask. Sexy as hell. With a smile that promised—

'Mal's going to carry on with the rounds and page us if there are any problems,' Nic said, breaking into her thoughts. 'I'll let him know if we go to Theatre.'

She flushed. 'Right.'

'I'm not checking up on the quality of your work,' he added, misinterpreting the reason for her high colour.

'I didn't for one moment think you were.'

He sighed. 'Oh, hell. Look, Lucy, we got off to a bad start. Let's just forget it and start again, shall we?'

Forget what? That kiss, or what he'd overheard, or the dressing-down he'd started to give her? The second two, she could do, but the memory of the kiss firmly refused to budge.

Even now, she could still feel his lips against hers. Worse, she wanted him to do it again. In a much more private situation...

She'd only just got herself back under control by the time they reached A and E. 'I'm Lucy Williams—you paged me to look at a patient with suspected placental abruption,' she said to the receptionist.

'Yes. Her name's Mrs Andrews—Liza Andrews. She's in room two,' the receptionist replied. 'Yvonne Roper's with her.'

'Thanks.' Lucy led the way to room two and knocked on the door.

Yvonne answered the knock. 'Thanks for coming, Dr Williams.'

'It's Lucy,' Lucy responded. 'Any time. This is Nic Alberici, the new consultant on River. Before we see the patient, what's the presentation?'

'She's in constant pain, her uterus is tender and tense, she's bleeding slightly—it's dark red and clotted—and she's starting to look shocky,' Yvonne said.

'Out of proportion to the loss?' Nic asked.

'Yes. Her blood pressure's low.'

He and Lucy exchanged a glance. There were other causes of bleeding in pregnancy, but the symptoms Yvonne had described sounded very like placental abruption.

'I'm not happy with the foetal heartbeat either,' Yvonne added. 'I think the baby's getting distressed.'

'Is the scanner here yet?' Nic asked.

'No. I'll chase it up.'

'Thanks. We'll go and see her,' Lucy said. She knocked on the door, walked in and introduced herself and Nic to Mrs Andrews. 'Yvonne tells me you're in pain and you're losing blood. Would you mind if we examined you?'

'Please. Anything. Just don't let me lose my baby,' Liza Andrews whispered brokenly. 'I'm forty-three. It's my first baby. We waited so long, and if I lose him…' She choked. 'I might not be able to have another.'

'We'll do our best,' Lucy reassured her. 'There are lots of reasons for bleeding in pregnancy so don't assume it's the worst.' Lucy glanced at the observation chart. 'Your baby's heartbeat is still pretty regular, though your blood pressure's a bit low so we'll get some blood into you to help. Yvonne, can you cross-match and get me four units of O-neg?' she asked as the nurse came back in.

'We're waiting for the portable scanner to arrive,' she told Liza, 'then we'll be able to check what's going on a bit better. It might be just that your placenta's low-lying, what we call placenta praevia, so I'm not going to give you a vaginal examination.' If it was placenta praevia rather than an abruption, a vaginal exam could cause a catastrophic bleed. 'But I will give you some oxygen to help you breathe more easily.' She unhooked the mask from the wall. 'Just breathe in through this and try to relax.' She set the output at fifteen litres a minute. 'OK?'

Liza nodded.

Lucy gently examined the woman's abdomen.

'That hurts,' Liza said, taking the mask off her face.

'I'm sorry,' Lucy said. 'The good news is that your baby's lying normally.' She mouthed to Nic, 'I'm almost certain it's an abruption.'

Nic nodded and took Liza's hand. 'It says here you're thirty-six weeks.'

Liza's face screwed up in anguish. 'And it's too early for the baby to come!'

'It's quite normal for babies to arrive at thirty-seven weeks—so a few days earlier really isn't as bad as it sounds,' Nic reassured her, smiling. 'You're in the right place.'

'So my baby's going to be all right?'

'We'll do our best,' Lucy said, gently settling the oxygen mask back in place. She listened to the baby's heartbeat and didn't like what she heard. Nic was watching her face and she gave him a very brief shake of her head to let him know.

Yvonne arrived with the scanner in tow and the units of blood. Lucy quickly set up an intravenous infusion while Nic put the scanner in place.

'Lucy,' he said quietly.

She took one look at the screen and her heart sank. The placenta wasn't low-lying. And as Liza Andrews hadn't been visibly losing that much blood, the chances were that most of the blood from the abruption was trapped, known as a 'concealed abruption'.

'Mrs Andrews, you have what we call placental abruption,' Lucy said. 'It means that your placenta's started to come away from the wall of your womb.'

Liza blenched. 'Am I going to lose the baby?'

'Not if we can help it. But it's too big for me to let you go home again,' Lucy said. 'And I don't want to take any risks with the baby.'

'I'd like to deliver the baby by Caesarean section,' Nic said.

'Now?' Liza asked, horrified.

'Now,' Nic said. They could have given Liza tocolytic

drugs to stop the contractions, then medication to help mature the baby's lungs, but from Liza's symptoms they knew the abruption was big. The baby needed at least half the placenta to be attached and functioning, so they couldn't take the risk of leaving it.

'But—why me? Why now?'

'We don't know the causes,' said Lucy, 'but it's more common if you've had high blood pressure, you're an older mum or you have twins or triplets, you're a smoker or you take cocaine.'

Liza smiled weakly. 'I've never smoked or done drugs. I haven't even have a glass of wine since I found out I was pregnant, let alone anything else!'

'That's good,' Lucy said, squeezing her hand.

'Have you been in a car accident or had a fall, or banged your stomach in any way?' Nic asked.

Liza shook her head. 'Not that I can remember.'

'We'll take some blood for tests to see why it's happened,' Lucy said, 'and to check that your blood's clotting properly.' If Liza Andrews had lost a lot of blood, she might have clotting problems after the birth, known as DIC or disseminated intravascular coagulation—around a third of cases did. And she had a much higher risk of a large bleed after delivery, so she might need a transfusion. 'We might need to give you some drugs to help your uterus contract after the birth.'

Liza nodded.

'And because your baby's early, we'll need to take him—or her—to the special care unit for a little while, to help him with his breathing and feeding. But you'll be able to see the baby any time you like,' Nic said.

'Is there anyone you'd like us to call?' Lucy asked.

'My husband's already on his way in. And my mum.' Liza's eyes filled with tears. 'He wanted to cut the cord.'

'I'm sorry,' Nic said. 'I'll need to give you a general anaesthetic, so he won't be allowed in for the delivery. But as soon as the baby arrives, he'll be able to have a cuddle.'

A tear slid down to pool on the mask. 'It was all supposed to be so different.'

'I know,' Lucy soothed. 'Though you're not alone. This happens in around one in fifty pregnancies.' Not all abruptions were as severe as this one—if the baby wasn't in distress and the bleed was minor, the mum could often go home if she chose. 'But you'll have your baby very soon.' She just hoped the abruption wasn't so severe that the baby wasn't getting enough oxygen—it could suffer brain death or even die.

'I'd like you to sign a consent form, please,' Nic said.

'I'll call the anaesthetist and get Theatre to prep,' Lucy said.

On their way up to Theatre, Nic said, 'You handled that well. It's a rough situation.'

'Let's just hope she doesn't get renal failure or a bad PPH,' Lucy said, referring to postpartum haemorrhage, a major bleed after delivery. She couldn't bring herself to talk about the risks to the baby.

Before she knew it, they were in Theatre and Nic was making the first incision. Lucy couldn't believe how fast he worked, but she was relieved when she was finally able to lift the baby out. 'It's a girl,' she said.

'Welcome, *bellissima*,' Nic said softly. His eyes crinkled at the corners, betraying the smile behind his surgeon's mask, and he handed her to Lucy. 'What's the Apgar score, Lucy?' he asked as he delivered the placenta and started stitching—the Apgar score was a check on the baby's pulse, breathing, whether the skin was pink or blue and the baby's reaction to suction.

'First Apgar score of five,' Lucy said, checking the baby.

She gave the baby gentle suction to clear her airways. Her skin wasn't pink enough either for Lucy's liking.

'Second score of seven,' she reported four minutes later.

The ten-minute score had improved to nine. 'But this little scrap's going to up to SCBU—' the special care baby unit '—to warm up for a bit,' Lucy said.

Nic finished closing. 'We'll leave Liza in the recovery team's capable hands and baby Andrews to SBCU.' He glanced at the clock. 'And we're going to have some lunch.'

Lunch? He wanted to have lunch with her? Her stomach fluttered at the idea of it. Lunch. Sitting opposite him on one of the small cafeteria tables, close enough for their knees to touch...

Way, way too dangerous. 'Thanks for the offer, but I'd better get back to the ward,' she said. 'Finish the rounds— it's not fair on Mal. One of us ought to go back and you did all the tough work in Theatre, so you deserve the break. I don't think I've ever seen a scalpel move that fast.'

Coward, his eyes said. 'Maybe Mal needs to feel you trust him enough to finish the rounds on his own.'

And maybe Nic ought to get to know the staff properly before he started throwing his weight about. Just because he'd got the consultant's job, it didn't mean he knew everything. She knew Mal far better than he did. She lifted her chin. 'Maybe I don't feel he's ready.'

'Lunch first,' Nic said.

'I really need to get back.' *Liar*, a voice in her head taunted. *You'd love to have lunch with him. And more.*

Given her track record at judging the men in her life, that'd be a very bad move. Anyway, she doubted if he meant *that* sort of lunch. He was her boss, not her lover.

Despite that kiss.

'I want to get to know all the team,' Nic said, 'and I thought I might as well start with you.'

So he *was* thinking of her as a doctor, nothing else. Just part of the team. He was going to ask everyone else to lunch, too. He hadn't singled her out as special. But she still couldn't help thinking about that kiss. He hadn't mentioned it, but was he remembering the way it had been between them, that unlooked-for spark at the ball when their mouths had touched?

'So, shall we?'

Before Lucy could open her mouth to refuse—or, worse, accept—her pager bleeped. She glanced at the display.

'Sorry. I'm needed back on the ward. Catch you later,' she said, hoping she sounded as casual as he had when he'd told her he wanted to get to know the team. And without giving him the chance to answer, she strode swiftly away.

CHAPTER TWO

COOL, calm, very English—and clearly as mad as hell at him.

And Nic couldn't blame her, in the circumstances. He'd taken her job and he'd embarrassed her at the ball in front of all her colleagues...and friends? Nic wasn't sure, yet, if Lucy Williams believed in friends.

She certainly didn't believe in lovers. The shock on her face when he'd kissed her had told him that.

What he couldn't work out was why. Why a woman who was clever and talented—enough to take on the role of acting consultant at the very young age of thirty—and beautiful wasn't already spoken for. No, scratch the beautiful—she was more than that. She looked like an angel, with that alabaster skin and those clear blue eyes and the ice-blonde hair pulled back severely from her face—hair he wanted to see tumbling down over her shoulders or, better still, over his pillow. Her mouth was a perfect rosebud and he just hadn't been able to resist kissing her at the ball.

And then she'd vanished. He'd looked for her immediately after the next dance, but she'd gone.

And then, when she'd faced him on the ward...

He took a swig of coffee. Leave her alone. That would be the sensible thing to do. Anything else would be breaking all his rules, professional and private.

Except...he couldn't.

'Down, boy,' he said softly to his libido.

It didn't take the slightest bit of notice.

* * *

20

Lucy somehow managed to avoid Nic for the rest of her shift. Usually she stayed later than she needed to, because the team on River was overstretched and she didn't mind giving up her free time. She loved her job. But today she needed to get as far away from Nic Alberici as she could. Until she'd managed to get her hormones under control and could treat him with detached professionalism.

The next day, she thought she'd managed it.

Until Nic walked into the side-room where she was talking to Liza Andrews.

'Mr Alberici.' Liza was beaming. 'Thanks so much for what you did for us yesterday—you and Dr Williams. You saved our lives.'

'Pleasure,' Nic said. 'How are you both today?'

'Tired, but fine. Lucy sleeps all the time.'

Nic cast a quizzical look at his senior reg.

'This Lucy,' Lucy explained, still holding the sleeping baby.

'We called her after you both—Lucy Nicola,' Liza told him.

'Thank you. It's an honour,' he said quietly. He stroked the baby's cheek. 'She's beautiful.'

'And Rosemary says the white stuff on her skin—vernix—will wash off in a couple of days.'

'When they're overdue it goes the other way—they're like little, wrinkled old men with very dry skin and you go through tons of moisturiser,' Nic said.

To Lucy's horror, he actually sat down on the arm of the chair she was using. Not quite close enough to touch—but close enough for her to feel his body heat. Why couldn't he have sat in the chair on the other side of the bed? Why did he have to invade her space like this?

'My turn for a cuddle,' he said, holding his arms out.

For one heart-stopping moment, she thought he meant a cuddle with *her*. But, of course, he meant baby Lucy.

'You're worse than the midwives—want to keep the babies all to yourselves,' he teased.

'I'd better get on anyway,' she said, gently transferring her tiny bundle into his arms and making sure that the baby's head was supported.

You're avoiding me, his eyes accused.

Tough, hers said back. 'Bye, Liza. Catch you later, Nic,' she said a lot more casually than she felt, and left the little room. Why did he have to look so—so *sexy*, holding baby Lucy?

'Get a grip,' she warned herself, and went to check the file of her next patient.

But her avoidance strategy didn't last long. She'd seen two more patients when Mal met her in the corridor. 'Boss wants a word with you,' he said.

'What about?'

'Dunno. He did say as soon as you could manage it.' He gave her a wicked grin. 'What have you been up to, Luce?'

'Working, Malcolm,' she said, clearly a shade too defensively because his grin broadened.

'I'll believe you, Luce.'

Lucy decided not to dignify him with a reply and went down the corridor to Nic's office. She rapped on the door.

'Come in.'

She put her head round the door. 'You wanted a word?'

He nodded. 'Come in and close the door, please.'

Her heart sank. What was she supposed to have done now?

He waited for her to sit down, and the knot in her stomach tightened. She hadn't done anything wrong. So why did she feel as if she were about to be carpeted for some stupid mistake? The tension in the room grew until she wanted to scream.

And then he smiled at her. 'I wanted to apologise,' he said, 'for embarrassing you at the ball the other night.'

She stared at him in disbelief. He was *apologising*?

'If you want to slap my face, feel free—any time,' he said, shocking her further. Did this mean that kiss *hadn't* been a set-up? But, given what she now knew about him, thanks to an old friend she'd trained with, he could be teasing her again.

There was only one way to find out. 'Why did you do it?'

'Kiss you?' He gave her a wry smile. 'Why do you think?'

'You always have to rise to a challenge.' The words were out before she could stop them.

'Something like that.'

So it *had* been a set-up. She lifted her chin. 'Then you're very easily manipulated. And you'll find certain junior staff more than willing to take advantage of that.'

He frowned. 'I'm not with you.'

'If someone dares you to do something, you'll just do it?' She rolled her eyes.

'Dares me to do what?'

It was her turn to frown. Weren't they talking about the same thing? 'You were dared to kiss me at the ball.'

Lucy thought someone had set him up him to kiss her? Nic just about managed to stop his jaw dropping. She really had that low an opinion of herself? But why? Didn't she know how gorgeous she was? 'Lucy...it wasn't like that,' he said carefully.

'Wasn't it?'

'No.'

'So why did you kiss me, then?'

'Because I wanted to.' He tipped his head on one side. 'Why do you think I was *dared* to do it?'

'Because…'

The words clearly stuck in her throat. Though he could guess what she was going to say. His brief getting-to-know-the-team conversation with Rosemary had told him an awful lot more than the senior midwife realised. Especially about Lucy. Which meant he had to handle this carefully.

'You looked as if you wanted to be a thousand miles away,' he said. 'I wanted to…' He lapsed into Italian.

'Sorry. Latin, yes, as long as it's medical—Italian, no,' Lucy said.

He smiled wryly. 'I said I wanted make you smile. It was all meant to be a bit of fun. Theatrical.'

'It was that all right,' she said drily.

Until their mouths had actually touched. Then it had become a whole new ballgame. A much, much more serious thing. He couldn't help looking at her mouth now. Big mistake. It reminded him how she'd tasted. And he wanted to do it again. And again. Somewhere they wouldn't be disturbed.

Here, a little voice said inside his head. *Here and now. Your office door is closed…*

He should be detached and professional. He was her colleague—a colleague who'd taken the job she'd been doing for weeks. So he was supposed to be treading on eggshells. He was supposed to keep his distance. He knew all that. And in spite of it, he found himself walking round to her side of the desk. Taking her hand. Turning it palm uppermost… And she didn't pull away.

'I wanted to kiss you, Lucy,' he said. 'I wanted to…' The touch of her skin was too much for him. All his good intentions went straight out of the window. Unable to help

himself, he bent his head and kissed the inside of her wrist.
'I wanted to do this,' he said huskily.

Nic's Italian. A showman. A flirt. For goodness' sake, you
know what Pauline told you yesterday—the corridors at
Plymouth hospital are littered with broken hearts. *He's a
brilliant doctor and great to work with—but don't be stupid
enough to go out with him. He never dates anyone more
than three times.*

What's he's doing to you doesn't mean a thing, Lucy
warned herself frantically. That smouldering smile's just a
performance. As soon as you let him sweep you off your
feet, you'll have two more dates and then he'll be off to
the next challenge.

Her body wasn't buying it. It went completely un-doctor-
like. Her pulse quickened, her pupils expanded and she
could feel her face growing bright red. 'I...'

'And this,' he said, touching his tongue to the pulse that
had started to beat crazily against her skin.

'And—' The harsh sound of his bleeper cut across his
words.

'Saved by the bleep,' he said wryly, taking his pager
from his pocket and glancing at the display. 'But I think
we need to talk, Lucia *mia.*'

Lucy stayed sitting exactly where she was as he left the
room. What on earth was going on? She was the sensible
one in the family—apart from the one huge mistake in her
life that nobody ever talked about, she'd always been sensible and studious and never let anything get in the way of
her work. She hardly knew Nic Alberici, only what she'd
heard about him from her friend Pauline in Nic's old hospital—that professionally he was wonderful and personally
he was a walking disaster area.

So why was her body reacting to him like this? Why did

her pulse race when she heard his voice or saw his smile? Why did her body go up in flames every time he touched her?

Why had he kissed the inside of her wrist like that?

And as for the way he'd Italianised her name—well, she wasn't a glamorous and sexy Lu-chee-ah. She was sensible Lucy Williams, senior registrar. She wore sensible, comfortable shoes and tailored trousers to work; she kept her hair pinned back severely, never wore nail-varnish and her make-up was non-existent. Lucia, on the other hand, would be tall and elegant. She'd wear a little black skirt and kitten heels, with her dark pre-Raphaelite curls tumbling down her back, her dark eyes outlined with sexily smudged kohl and her lips with kiss-me-now red lipstick.

Lucy Williams wasn't the sort of woman Nic Alberici wanted, and she wasn't going to forget that. She wasn't going to have some wild fling with him that would last no more than three dates anyway; she wasn't stupid enough to think she was the one who could change him. She'd learned at a very young age that happy-ever-after didn't exist. The one time she'd been tempted to take a risk had taught her only too painfully that she'd been right all along—and her judgement in men was rotten.

Lucia mia. The words made her heart miss a beat. And a second.

Don't be stupid, she reminded herself. You're not his. Nothing's going to come of it. Next time you see him, you're going to tell him to leave you alone.

'You haven't had a break for five hours.'

A shiver ran down her spine; Nic's voice was like a caress on her skin.

Don't be ridiculous, Lucy, she told herself crossly. 'I'm fine,' she snapped.

'You need a break. So do I. And you know the hospital better than I do—you can show me where to find some decent coffee instead of the stewed stuff I had at lunchtime.'

'I can tell you where to go.'

He grinned, deliberately misinterpreting her. 'I'll bet.'

'I don't need a break, Mr Alberici.'

'OK—then I'll pull rank, Dr Williams. Coffee. With me. Now.'

She walked in silence with him out of the ward, aware of the speculative looks cast their way and determined not to give anyone the excuse to gossip about her. She remained silent until they were well out of earshot of the ward.

'I'd like you to leave me alone in future,' she said. 'What you did in your office—' *made my knees go weak again* '—was sexual harassment,' she finished stiffly. 'I'd prefer you not to repeat it.'

He nodded and his face became impassive. 'In future, Lucy, I'll make sure I have your permission before I touch you.'

It was what she wanted. So why did his words make her feel as if the sun had stopped shining?

And why was he going to drag her through the torment of having coffee with him?

'Though I prefer to be on friendly terms with my colleagues,' he said.

Yeah, right. Three dates and you're out.

'So perhaps we should put all this behind us.'

'As you wish.' Lucy gave him a cool nod.

'So, where are we having this coffee?'

She seized the chance to change the subject, turn it to something more neutral. 'Pat's Place, on the second floor. The mochaccino's to die for. Not to mention the blueberry muffins—Pat makes them herself. Pat's the one with the dangly earrings.'

Shut up *now*, Lucy. You're babbling, she told herself.

Not that Nic seemed to mind. There wasn't a trace of impatience in his tone. 'Blueberry muffins, hmm? A woman after my own heart,' he said.

She wasn't anything of the sort. The man was a born flirt. And anyway, he was just trying to find common ground with a member of his new team, she reminded herself.

The walk to the coffee-bar was torture. With every step, she remembered the way he'd touched her. The way her skin had heated as he'd turned her palm over. The way his lips had brushed her skin, sending tingles down her spine. The way he'd licked her pulse point...

She glanced down quickly, relieved that her white coat was thick enough to hide the obvious signs of her arousal. Hell. She couldn't let this happen. Not again. And she absolutely refused to let herself believe that Nic was different. She'd leave that line to her mother and her three sisters. Susie, Allie, Mum and Rach—every time they convinced themselves that 'this one's different' and he never was.

As for Nic Alberici, Pauline had told her he was a heart-breaker—and what reason would one of her best friends from med school have to lie to her? No, Nic Alberici was just the same as all the rest. Love 'em and leave 'em. She should stay well clear.

He's gorgeous, the voice in her head insisted.

That's irrelevant, she told herself. Looks don't come into it.

But you want to—

'Lucy?'

She'd been so intent on arguing with herself she hadn't heard a word he'd said. 'Sorry. I didn't catch what you said,' she mumbled, embarrassed at being caught wool-gathering.

'Mochaccino and a muffin?'

'Yes, please.'

'Grab us a table. These are on me.'

She was about to protest that she'd pay for her own, but his eyes warned her it'd be better to accept with good grace. 'Thanks,' she said.

She found a small table in the corner. He joined her with a tray of coffee and muffins.

This is his part-of-the-team chat, she reminded herself. So let's keep it work-related. 'Settled in OK to Treverro?' she asked.

He nodded. 'They're a nice bunch on River.'

'Yes.'

'Spit it out,' he said, surprising her.

'Spit what out?'

'You're obviously dying to take me to task.'

'I don't know what you mean.'

He grinned. 'Lucy, your eyes go all schoolmarmy when you're annoyed about something.'

Did they? She'd never realised she was so transparent.

'You are to me,' he said softly, and she realised she'd spoken aloud.

'Nonsense,' she said crisply.

'So what am I doing wrong?'

'Nothing.'

'Explain the schoolmarmy look, then.'

Well, he was asking for it… 'You're right about the staff on River. They're a nice bunch and I'd hate to see them hurt,' she informed him.

'You think *I'd* hurt them?' He frowned. 'Why?'

'You have a reputation.'

He rolled his eyes. 'Oh, not that Italian playboy stuff

again! Lucy, I'm not a stereotype. Yes, I like to have fun— but I stick to the rules and no one gets hurt. Just take me as I am.'

Her libido fluttered and she stamped on it hard. Don't go getting any ideas, she warned it. 'Yes, boss.'

His lips thinned. 'If you don't believe me, ask yourself if *your* reputation's deserved.'

She didn't need to ask him which reputation. She was all too aware of it. 'My career's important to me.'

'But that doesn't make you a cold fish.'

She knew that. Her patients did, too. And as for the men she'd turned down—they just needed to grow up enough to realise they weren't irresistible and it didn't mean she was a challenge to be conquered. Her reputation didn't bother her.

'Or any less of a woman,' Nic added softly, and her insides melted at the flash of sensuality in his eyes.

This conversation was definitely straying onto worrying territory. She sat up straighter. 'My private life's just that.'

'And so is mine.'

'Good. Then we're agreed.'

He spread his hands. 'Lucy, why are we fighting?'

'Because...' Her voice faded. She didn't know why she was fighting Nic. She couldn't even remember the last time she'd rowed with a colleague. Bickering with Mal was different because it wasn't *personal* and the SHO reminded her of one of her kid brothers, and she didn't find Mal remotely attractive. Whereas Nic...

No. Focus. Career first, last and always, she reminded herself.

'Because I kissed you?' His voice grew husky. 'It was before I knew who you were. And, yes, I lost it a bit in my office this afternoon. I shouldn't have done what I did and I apologise. What can I do to make it up to you?'

Kiss me again.

Lucy prayed she hadn't said that out loud. She hadn't meant to think it either. And it had better not have shown on her face.

He took a sip of coffee, then broke off a piece of blueberry muffin.

Since when had eating cake been sexy? Lucy tried very hard to stop looking at his mouth. Or remembering what his lips had felt like against her skin.

'This is good,' he told her.

'Mmm.' She took refuge in her own coffee. Though she'd lost her appetite for her blueberry muffin. It was too dangerous. She'd already had to yank her thoughts away from the idea of Nic feeding her morsels of cake as he—

No!

'Why are you so anti-relationship?' Nic asked without warning.

Lucy almost choked on her coffee. 'I beg your pardon?'

'Being committed to your job doesn't mean you have to spend your life alone,' he said. 'So what's the real story?'

'You've got a nerve!'

'I just want to know what makes you tick. You're my number two in the department,' he reminded her. 'The most important member of my team.'

'All right, since you want to know.' She folded her arms. 'Both my parents are on their fourth marriages, all my brothers and sisters are divorced and I don't see the point of wasting all that emotion when I could use the energy much more effectively in my work.'

'Who says you'll go the same way?'

'Because there's a pattern.'

'You could be the one to change it.'

She wasn't. Jack Hammond was living proof. Not that she was going to tell Nic about *him*. Nobody at Treverro knew about Jack, and she wanted to keep it that way. 'I'm not. And you're in no position to lecture me, anyway.'

'No?'

'Has anyone lasted more than three dates with you?' She waited for a moment. 'If you have to think that hard about it, clearly not many have.'

'You know when you meet the right one,' he said.

Lucy scoffed. 'Come off it. Don't the statistics show that one in three marriages end in divorce?'

'Which leaves two in three that don't.'

'So you're telling me you believe in happy-ever-after?'

He nodded. 'Since you believe in patterns, there's one in my family. My parents had a holiday romance—they didn't even speak the same language when they first met—but my father followed my mother back to England and they've been married for more than forty years. And they're still in love. My sisters are both happily married—Gina for fifteen years and Sofia for twelve.'

'So why aren't you following their pattern?'

'Because I'm waiting for the right one.'

'And that's your excuse for a trail of broken hearts?'

'That's an exaggeration, Lucy. Do you expect your date to propose to you at the end of the first evening?'

'Of course not.'

'Exactly. If I go out with someone, it's to have a good time and we both know the rules right from the start. I'm not a heart-breaker—and you're not frozen.'

That look in his eyes was back. The one that made her insides smoulder. This really wasn't fair. 'What's Nic short for?' she asked, desperate to change the subject.

'Niccolo.'

'As in Machiavelli?'

He grinned. 'Yup. But I'm not manipulative.'

'No?'

'I didn't manipulate you into telling me things. Just as I'm not going to manipulate you into bed.'

That feeling flooding through her spine was *not* disappointment, she told herself. 'Good,' she said tightly. 'So we know where we stand.'

'I'm attracted to you, Lucy,' he said softly. 'Very. I'd like to get to know you better—a *lot* better—outside work. But you've made it clear you're not interested, and I'm not going to push you into something you're not comfortable with.'

'Good,' she said again, even though her heart was wailing *You idiot!* and doing the mental version of foot-stamping and hair-tearing.

'So we're colleagues. I'd like to think we can be friends, too.'

'Of course.'

'Good.' Nic finished his muffin. 'Aren't you going to eat yours?'

'I'm not hungry.'

'Would you mind if I...?'

She pushed the plate over to him. 'Help yourself.'

'It's my mum's fault. I have this weakness for cake,' he said.

'I'll remember that,' she said lightly.

He hadn't taken more than a mouthful before his bleeper sounded. He glanced down at the display and raised an eyebrow. 'What do you know about TOPS?'

'Twin oligohydramnios-polyhydramnios sequence—also known as twin-to-twin transfusion syndrome,' she said.

'Good. I prefer to call it twin-to-twin transfusion—it's more of a parent-friendly explanation. We're needed downstairs in the antenatal clinic,' he said. 'Now.'

CHAPTER THREE

THEY left their unfinished coffee and headed for the ground floor. Gemma Burton, one of the midwives, gave them the case notes and directed them to room two. Nic scanned them swiftly, gave them to Lucy to do the same, knocked on the door and introduced them both to Molly Drake.

'How have you been feeling?' he asked, sitting next to her and holding her hand.

'OK—but then last week I started to feel a bit breathless. And I look like a house—I'm only seventeen weeks and I look like I'm going to deliver any day,' she said. Her faced was pinched with anxiety. 'I know I'm having twins but I never expected to be this big. And my tummy's felt really tight in the last day or so.'

'Would you mind if I examined you?' Nic asked.

'No. I just want to know, are my babies all right? The midwife said she wanted the consultant to see me...'

'Hey, we always take extra special care of our mums having twins, so you'd get to see me a lot more often than mums of single babies anyway,' Nic said reassuringly. 'But, yes, I'm a bit concerned that you've put on weight very quickly and you're breathless. I'd like to do a scan to see what's going on, if I may?'

Molly nodded.

It didn't take long for Nic to do the scan and see that his worst fears were realised. One twin was much bigger than the other. It had a full bladder, whereas the other twin's bladder was empty, and the smaller twin seemed almost stuck to the wall of the placenta—which, he knew, meant that it had much less amniotic fluid in the sac surrounding it.

'Is everything all right?' Molly asked.

Nic held her hand again. 'There's a bit of a problem, but the good news is that we can do something about it. You have something called TTTS or twin-to-twin transfusion syndrome.'

'What's that?'

Nic gestured at Lucy. 'Over to you, Lucy.'

'It's something that happens when identical twins share the same placenta,' Lucy said. 'Their blood vessels form a link in the placenta—most of the time that isn't a problem, but sometimes the link isn't balanced properly, so one twin ends up donating blood to the other. The babies are perfectly normal—the problem's in the placenta. We don't know exactly why it happens, but it might be to do with how late the fertilised egg splits to create two embryos. It happens in around one in a thousand pregnancies.'

'And that's what's wrong with my babies?' Molly asked.

Lucy nodded and turned the ultrasound screen so that Molly could see it. 'You can see on the scan here that one twin's a lot bigger than the other. If we measure their lengths, it looks as if this one's a week older than his twin, even though we know he's not. The bigger twin has too much blood going round his system, so his heart has to work harder, and he produces more amniotic fluid—that's the bag of fluid the baby lives in—so he wees more and his bladder's full. The smaller twin is anaemic and has less amniotic fluid surrounding him; he doesn't grow as well and his bladder's usually empty.'

'Are they going to be all right? What—what can do you do to stop it?'

'There are quite a few options,' Nic said. 'We can do something called amnioreduction—that means draining some of the fluid from around the bigger twin, which gives the smaller twin more space in the womb and will make you feel a lot more comfortable. It also reduces the chance of you going into premature labour. If we do that, it takes about an hour and we drain off two to three litres of fluid. I'd also like you to stay in hospital for a day or so, so we can monitor you, and then you can go back home, as long as you promise to stay in bed and take it easy for a few days.' He squeezed her hand. 'Though if you do take this option, we might need to repeat it later in your pregnancy, depending on how things go with the twins.'

'There's also something called a septostomy, where we make a little hole in the membrane that separates the twins and the fluid balances out between the sacs—we often do that at the same time as an amnioreduction,' Lucy said. 'Or we can send you to a hospital in London for laser treatment, which will break the joined blood vessels and stop the blood going from one twin to the other—it won't hurt them and they'll be able to grow normally. There's another new treatment being tested at the moment which involves high-frequency ultrasound therapy—the same sort that's used to treat kidney stones—though again if you choose this we'll have to send you to a centre in London, as we can't do it here.'

'And the babies will both be all right?'

'We've caught you relatively early, which is a good sign,' Nic said. 'If they both survive, the smaller twin should catch up on growth after the birth. But at this stage I can't guarantee they'll both be fine.'

'So they might die?'

'I know it's a horrible thing to have to consider, but there's a possibility you might lose one or both of them. I can't quote any odds at this stage, and we'll monitor you a lot more often than we'd usually plan and make sure we do everything we can to keep your babies safe,' Nic reassured her. 'There are two other options you need to think about, and I'm afraid they're not very pleasant, but you need to know all the facts before you can make a decision. Some parents opt to have a termination now, because they feel the odds are stacked too high against them. I know it's an unbearable thing to think about, but if you decide that's what you want, we're not going to judge you or criticise you.'

'We're here to give you the facts and to support you, whatever decision you make,' Lucy said. 'We're on your side.'

'I...' Molly was clearly close to tears and Lucy handed her a tissue.

'The other option, if we find that the procedures don't work and the twin-to-twin transfusion is getting worse, is that we might be able to save one twin at the expense of the other,' Nic said. 'I know it sounds callous, but it's a question of weighing up the risks.'

'But you and your partner really need to discuss it and decide what you want,' Lucy added.

'George isn't here,' Molly said. 'He's away in the States on business. He said he'd change his meetings if I needed him here today, but I thought this'd be just...well, a routine visit.'

'I know.' Lucy brought a chair to the other side of the bed and held Molly's other hand. 'And this must have come as a shock to you. Is there anyone we can call to be with you?'

Molly shook her head. 'I'm not on good terms with my parents, and George's mum panics at the least little thing— she's the last person I need fluttering round me. I just...' She bit her lip hard. 'Twins. When we found out, we never thought we'd cope. We'd just got used to the idea and started getting excited about it, and now this!'

'Take your time,' Nic said. 'I'd like to start treatment in the next twenty-four hours—but if you want to talk to your husband or a friend first, discuss it with them, that's fine.'

'Would you explain the options to my husband?' Molly asked Lucy.

'Of course,' Lucy said. 'There's no pressure. Take all the time you need. Can I get you some water or anything?'

'It's all right. It's just a shock. I need to think—I need to talk to George.' She swallowed. 'I can't use a mobile in here, can I?'

'No, it might interfere with the machines,' Lucy said. 'But I can take you somewhere where you can use it.'

'Thanks.'

She looked at Nic. 'See you back on the ward?'

'Yeah.' Nic smiled at Molly. 'We're here whenever you need us. If either of us isn't on duty, just ask someone to bleep us. We'll be straight here.'

Four hours later, Lucy was sitting in the rest room and trying very hard not to cry. She'd held Molly's hand throughout the difficult call to the States, and the even more difficult decision that had followed.

Molly had been admitted to the ward and Lucy was well past the time when she was supposed to finish her shift, but her vision was blurred with suppressed tears and she didn't feel quite up to cycling back to her cottage.

'Are you OK, Lucy?'

Lucy looked up and gave Nic a watery smile. 'I thought you were supposed to be off duty ages ago.'

'I'm not the only one.' He came to sit next to her. 'It's Molly Drake, isn't it?' he guessed.

She nodded. 'I know, I know, these cases are rare and

most of the time our mums have a healthy pregnancy and a healthy baby—but I hate to see the heartbreak some of our parents have to go through.'

'Me, too,' Nic said. 'But remember this—we can make a difference. We *do* make a difference.'

'Yes. Molly's having a septostomy tomorrow and we'll be monitoring her weekly. The twins stand a much better chance now.'

'Chin up.' He gave her an exaggerated wink, then sent her hormones into overdrive by gently touching her cheek. 'Go on. Home with you. And I'll see you tomorrow.'

Lucy slept badly that night; when she did drift off, her dreams were filled with Nic Alberici. And they were so graphic that she was actually blushing when her alarm went off.

When she got to work, she seemed to hear nothing but Nic's name. Every single patient beamed when they talked about him—all saying he was far dishier than any Hollywood star and acting as if they were half in love with him. The midwives were similarly smitten—the young and single ones virtually swooned when they heard his name, and the older ones clucked over him like a favourite son. 'He's lovely—a real gentleman,' Rosemary said dreamily. 'And those gorgeous eyes! If I were twenty years younger…'

'Oh, he's just another consultant,' Lucy said, aware how grumpy she sounded and hoping that no one would pick up on it.

No chance. Rosemary's eyes widened. 'Have you two had a fight or something?'

'No. It's just a bit wearing hearing how fantastic Mr Alberici is—almost as wearing as Mal's sense of humour. Even the mums who've had a difficult delivery say they'd like another baby right now, please, if it means they'll have Mr Alberici looking after them.'

Rosemary whistled. 'Someone got out on the wrong side of the bed this morning, didn't she?'

If she said anything else, it'd start the hospital rumour mill whirring. 'Yeah, probably,' Lucy said, and switched the topic back to work.

Though she couldn't get Nic out of her mind. She was aware of exactly when he walked onto the ward and exactly when he left. And she hated this out-of-control feeling. It's like you told Rosemary—he's just another consultant, she reminded herself.

Except she had a nasty feeling that he wasn't.

'I'm worried about this one,' Beth said, handing Lucy the notes of another patient. 'Judy Sutherland's diabetic and the baby's big. I think there's a high risk of shoulder dystocia.' Shoulder dystocia, also known as impacted shoulders, was where the baby's shoulders couldn't be delivered after the head had been delivered. It happened when the baby was large, overdue or had a short cord—babies of diabetic mothers had greater shoulder-to-chest ratios so they were particularly prone to it.

'Judy says she doesn't want a section under any circumstances,' Beth added.

'We might not have to give her a section. If you're right and the shoulders are impacted, we'll have to do the McRoberts manoeuvre,' Lucy said. That meant putting the mother into the lithotomy position with her buttocks supported on a pillow over the edge of the bed, then flexing her hips to make her pelvic outlet bigger, hopefully enough to deliver the baby. 'Then if we rotate the baby so his anterior shoulder is under the symphysis pubis, we should be OK. Though she'll need a large epidural and there's a possibility of problems with the baby—a fractured clavicle at the very least.' Erb's palsy, where the nerves in the arm were affected, was another possibility, and a third of babies affected by shoulder dystocia had permanent damage. She sighed. 'Do you want me to have a word with Judy and check she understands all the risks?'

'Or maybe we should ask Nic to do it,' Beth suggested. Lucy sighed inwardly as she saw the familiar glow in the midwife's face. Beth was clearly yet another member of the Niccolo Alberici fan club. 'He's so charming, she's bound to listen.'

'Yes, Nic's very charming, on the surface,' Lucy agreed, all sweetness and light and wanting to strangle the man.

'Nice of you to say so, Dr Williams.'

Lucy's eyes widened as she heard his voice. Her early warning system had just failed spectacularly, and again he'd caught her saying something outrageous. Gingerly, she turned to face Nic.

'There's a case I want to discuss with you in my office, Lucy,' he said. 'If you'd be so kind.'

'And then would you have a word with Mrs Sutherland for me, please, Nic?' Beth asked.

'Sure.' Nic gave her one of his trade-mark smiles, his eyes crinkling at the corners in a way that clearly made the midwife melt. 'Lucy?'

Sighing inwardly, she followed him into his office.

'Close the door, please,' he said.

Lucy did so.

'Take a seat.' He frowned. 'This is beginning to be a habit—me overhearing something you'd much rather I didn't.'

'Well, eavesdroppers never hear any good of themselves,' Lucy retorted.

'I thought we'd sorted out all the problems between us?'

She sighed. 'OK, OK, I'm sorry.'

He folded his arms. 'Not good enough.'

She couldn't read his expression. 'You'd prefer me to ask for a transfer?'

'No.'

'What, then?'

'Make it up to me.'

Her eyes narrowed with suspicion. 'What do you have in mind?'

'Spend the day with me tomorrow.'

'Spend the day with you tomorrow?' she echoed, surprised. That was the last thing she'd expected.

'Mmm-hmm. I'm a new boy in the area. I could do with a hand finding my feet. I want to explore the district and I'd like some company.'

Lucy scoffed. 'Why ask me? Talk to the midwives. And the nurses. And all the unattached female doctors. They're lining up in droves for you.'

He grinned. 'Oh, Lucia *mia*. You should know better than to believe the hospital rumour mill.'

She didn't dignify that with a reply.

'Lucy, I'm off duty tomorrow. So are you.'

How did he know? No, that was an easy one. All he had to do was look in the off-duty book.

'So spend the day with me, Lucy,' he coaxed. 'Show me the area.'

'You're perfectly capable of reading a map.'

'True. But it's not the same as playing tourist with someone who knows all the good spots.'

'Your idea of good spots might not be the same as mine.'

'On the other hand, they might be.'

Lucy shook her head. 'I don't think it's a good idea.'

'No strings, I promise.'

'Then two more dates and you'll leave me alone?' she asked hopefully.

Nic's eyes crinkled at the corners. 'We're not going on a date, Lucy.'

You couldn't get more crushing than that. She stared at the floor and wished herself a thousand miles away.

'We're merely spending the day together, as friends. Tell you what—I'll do you a deal. I'll talk your patient into being sensible over the shoulder dystocia issue and agreeing to a section if we find we have to do one for the baby's sake, and you can show me your favourite bits of north Cornwall.'

She opened her mouth to say no, but he didn't give her a chance to speak.

He laced his fingers together. 'I would suggest sealing the deal properly... But we're at work, and I promised I wouldn't touch you without your permission.' His eyes filled with mischief. 'It's a shame you're not a mind-reader. Then again, if you knew what I was thinking right now, you'd probably slap my face.'

'Don't tempt me.' Though her words were hollow. Just his mere existence tempted her. And she had a nasty feeling that she knew exactly what he was thinking. Sealing the deal with a kiss. Like the one at the fancy-dress ball—a kiss that might start out sweet and innocent but would heat up the minute their mouths met.

He said something in Italian and she folded her arms and glared at him.

'Translate.'

'I wouldn't dare.' He gave her a lazy grin. 'If you want to know what I said, you'll just have to learn Italian, won't you?'

It wasn't fair. Why did he have to have such a sensual mouth? And when he smiled like that, it made her want to act completely out of character. It made her want to reach over and kiss him. Passionately. And very, very improperly.

'Am I dismissed?' she asked.

'Are you going to spend tomorrow with me?'

'No,' she said crisply.

He clasped his hands theatrically to his heart. 'I tried.'

'You're very trying,' she snapped back.

He spread his hands. 'What can I say? The lady's always right.'

'I do have patients to see.'

'Then *arrivederci, Lucia mia*,' he said softly.

Corny, smarmy, pathetic... Oh, who was she trying to kid? That Italian accent was way, way too sexy for her peace of mind. Worse, she almost opened her mouth to say she'd changed her mind and, yes, she *would* spend the day with him.

Almost. Common sense prevailed. Just.

'You need your head tested, Lucy Williams,' she muttered to herself as she closed his office door.

Nic touched his mouth. No, it wasn't hot. And he hadn't kissed her, much as he'd wanted to. So why did he feel so scorched?

He smiled wryly. It was obvious: it had a lot to do with a certain Dr Williams and that beautiful rosebud mouth. It had taken all his self-control not to pull her into his arms and kiss her, make her feel that same blood-heating passion that zinged through his veins when he saw her.

Working with her was going to be torture.

Working with her was going to be heaven.

CHAPTER FOUR

THAT evening, Lucy found herself pacing her cottage, thinking about Nic.

'Stop it,' she told herself.

But she couldn't. Every time she closed her eyes, she could see his face. Smell his clean, masculine scent. Feel the sweetness of his mouth against hers.

Her day off was even worse. Supposing she hadn't been so stubborn—supposing she'd agreed to spend the day with him. It would have been a chance to get to know him better.

'You don't *want* to get to know him better,' she reminded herself. 'You want to be a top consultant. Your personal life's been a disaster zone for years. Stick to your career—it's safer.'

But what if? What if she'd gone to the beach with him? Supposing she'd taken him to Pentremain, her favourite place on earth, the tiny bay that was one of the best surfing sites in Europe and was spectacular in winter, with the waves crashing onto the rocks and the gulls wailing and the wind whipping roses into your cheeks... They'd have had lunch together in the tiny fishing port, at a secluded table overlooking the sea. Maybe another walk along the beach as the sun was setting.

And then a kiss...

Anyone would think she was a hormonal teenager, not a level-headed thirty-year-old! It was crazy, going weak at the knees at the thought of a kiss.

A kiss from a man who'd told her he felt the same attraction.

A kiss from a man who'd licked her pulse point and looked into her eyes and dared her not to believe how much he desired her.

If she didn't stop thinking about him, she'd go insane!

Well, there was one thing that would take her mind off him. Spring-cleaning. No matter that it was way out of season. Scrubbing every corner of her cottage would stop her thinking about him.

In theory. In practice, it didn't. So she chose the last resort. Cooking. Preferably something that would use up her energy and calm her down again. She didn't have any flour suitable for making bread, so that idea went out of the window...

Then she smiled. But she did have walnuts, honey and sesame seeds. Which meant she could knead out her frustration on a different sort of dough, still have that comforting breadmaking scent, and end up with something sweet to soothe her soul. *Kahk*, the recipe her Egyptian friend Noor had taught her when they'd shared a house in their second year of med school.

She ignored the fact that Nic had a thing about cake.

Or that the sweetness of the honeyed filling reminded her of his mouth.

'These are seriously good,' Nic said, taking a second sugar-dusted cake from the tin at the nurses' station the next morning. 'Icing sugar on the top. Not too sweet on the outside, but then you hit the inside... The mixture of textures and tastes is fabulous. Which mum do I need to thank—and beg to tell me where she bought them?'

'You don't,' Rosemary said.

'One of the staff brought them in?'

'Made by the fair hands of our own Lucy Williams.'

Rosemary winked. 'She's not just a pretty face and a good doctor, you know.'

You can say that again, Nic thought. I just wish she'd let me close enough to find out for myself.

'Hey, Lucy. You've got another convert to *kahk*,' Rosemary said.

Nic nearly choked on his cake. Since when had his radar stopped working and neglected to let him know that Lucy was in the same building, let alone a couple of feet away? He just about managed to retain his composure. 'Lucy, hi. These are very good. Unusual filling.'

'Walnuts, honey and sesame seeds,' she said.

And made by her. Was she still professional and orderly and neat when she cooked, or did she let her guard down? Did she push her hair out of her eyes and end up with a dusting of flour on the end of her nose? Did she filch bits of her favourite ingredients? Did those ice-blue eyes turn into the colour of sunny skies as she relaxed?

Nic had a vision of her in his kitchen, and himself removing her blue-and-white striped butcher's apron before—

'Are you all right, Nic?' Rosemary asked.

Hell. He'd actually moaned aloud at the thought of Lucy in very close proximity to him. He flushed and covered his confusion by taking a third piece. 'I have this thing about *dolci*—sweet things. And these are to die for. Oh-h-h,' he said, hamming it up and hoping that Rosemary hadn't guessed what he'd *really* been thinking about.

Making love with his registrar.

'You'll end up looking like our mums-to-be if you eat them at that rate—especially when it can't be more than half an hour since you had your breakfast,' Lucy informed him sweetly—then disappeared to see a patient before he could make an equally rude retort.

* * *

Well, I managed that OK, Lucy told herself. Cool, calm, even jokey.

But she still couldn't stop thinking about Nic. She was on autopilot when she answered the bleep from A and E asking her to see a pregnant holidaymaker who was bleeding, so she missed the patient's name. Until she saw the notes.

Nina Hammond.

Coincidence. It had to be. Hammond was hardly an uncommon surname, and Nina was a popular first name.

But the second she stepped into the cubicle and saw Nina's husband, she knew it wasn't a coincidence. It was the kind of nightmare that ripped open old wounds and then poured salt in them for good measure. Why, why, why hadn't she erred on the side of caution and let someone else deal with this?

But she was a professional. She wasn't going to let her ex see that she was affected by seeing him. Not in the slightest. 'Hello, Mr and Mrs Hammond,' she said, relieved that she was at least able to control the threatening tremor in her voice. 'I'm Lucy Williams, special registrar from the maternity unit.'

'Please, Dr Williams—don't let me lose my baby,' Nina Hammond said, clutching at Lucy's hand. 'Make it stop. Make the bleeding go away.'

'I'll do my best,' Lucy said, and took refuge in her clipboard as she took the patient history.

'We're on holiday,' Nina explained. 'We just wanted to spend some quiet time by the sea. We only got here yesterday. We were going for a drive round the coast—then I realised I was bleeding and Jack drove me straight here.'

'Someone's looking after your other children?' Lucy asked.

Nina shook her head. 'We don't have any.'

Shouldn't they have an older child—Lucy did a rapid mental calculation—one who was nearly four? Or maybe she'd got it wrong. She'd got a hell of a lot wrong where Jack was concerned.

'I've had three miscarriages,' Nina explained.

Lucy refused to meet Jack's eyes. 'I'm sorry to hear that. Has your GP sent you for any tests?'

'No. Should he have done?'

'If any of my patients lost three babies, I'd recommend further tests to see why,' Lucy said. 'It could be that your body's producing antibodies which make you miscarry, called antiphospholipid syndrome—if that's the case, we can give you something to help with that. Or maybe you have a problem with your cervix, and again that's something I can help with. But first of all, I'd like to examine you and do an ultrasound—a scan—to see what's going on. Are you losing much blood?'

'No—just spotting, really. I had cramps and I felt a bit of wetness and just panicked.' Nina bit her lip. 'I so want a baby. We've been trying for years. I've lost three babies already. If I lose this one, I...' She broke into sobs. 'I can't *bear* to go through all this again!'

'It's OK,' Lucy soothed. 'I'd like to take you up to my department—we can do a scan there and see what's going on, then maybe I'll admit you overnight so we can keep an eye on you and give things a chance to settle down.'

'Can my husband stay with me?'

Lucy took a deep breath. 'Let's cross that bridge when we come to it. I'll get a porter to bring you up to the ward and I'll meet you there—I'll have the equipment all set up to check you over. How many weeks are you, by the way?'

'Sixteen.'

Most women with antiphospholipid syndrome miscarried in the first trimester, so the most likely cause of Nina's miscarriages was either polycystic ovaries or an incompetent cervix, Lucy thought. 'Right, then, Mrs Hammond. I'll see you upstairs in a few minutes.'

She made a quick call to River to make sure a room was ready on the ward, then took the stairs back to the unit. The exercise helped calm her.

Jack Hammond. Tall, blond, blue-eyed and tanned. The kind of man who turned heads everywhere he walked. The kind of man women watched and sighed over. The kind of man who'd broken her heart into tiny, tiny shards that had taken her years to repair. She'd thought she'd never, ever see him again. After the messiest possible break-up, she'd moved down to Cornwall, where there'd be no memories to taunt her. She'd never, ever imagined that their paths would cross again.

She was back under control by the time she walked back into River Ward. Nina was waiting for her in one of the side rooms, still trembling and tearful.

'Can I get you a drink of water?' Lucy asked her.

'No, thanks. I think I'd be sick if I drank anything.' Nina clutched Jack's hand. 'My baby... Please, I need to know if my baby's all right.'

'Lift up your top and bare your tummy for me, and we'll see what's going on,' Lucy said gently. She set to work with the gel and the ultrasound scanner and soon had the picture she wanted on the screen.

She tilted the monitor so that Nina could see it. 'Can you see his heart beating there?' she said, pointing to the dark pulsating spot on the screen. 'It's nice and strong. He's given you a nasty scare but I'm pleased to say your baby's looking quite happy right now.'

'It's a boy?' Jack said.

'I can't tell from this angle. I don't like calling foetuses "it" so I call all the difficult ones "he",' Lucy said.

That one hit home, she thought with satisfaction as dark colour slid over Jack's cheekbones.

'Mrs Hammond, would it be all right if I examined you now?'

Nina nodded her consent, and Lucy examined her gently. 'I think you've got what's known as an incompetent cervix,' she said. 'It just means your cervix is shorter and thinner than it should be, so as the foetus gets bigger and heavier, the weight presses on your cervix, which opens earlier than it should do. The good news is, I can do something to help. I can put a stitch called a cerclage round your cervix to stop it opening too early; it acts almost like a purse-string and keeps your cervix closed. I'll need to do it under anaesthetic and keep you in on bed-rest for the next twenty-four hours, but it should hold your cervix closed for the rest of your pregnancy, and your doctor can remove it just before your due date.'

'So I won't lose my baby?'

'Hopefully not,' Lucy said. 'There are some side-effects with the procedure, such as bleeding or infection, but it'll give your baby more of a chance. You'll need to take it very easy for the rest of your pregnancy—your own doctor might even put you on full bed-rest until you have the baby—and I'm afraid you'll have to avoid vaginal intercourse for the rest of your pregnancy.'

'I see,' Jack said.

Lucy refused to look at him. Tough, she thought. You need to look after Nina, not think about your own selfish needs.

'If you feel anything like a contraction or you start leaking fluid, you should ring your midwife straight away,' she continued.

'I will,' Nina said. 'When can you put the stitch in?'

'Today,' Lucy said. 'When did you last have anything to eat?'

'Last night,' Nina told her. 'I couldn't face breakfast.'

'That's good. Don't eat or drink anything now, and I'll check when Theatre's free so I can take you up there. I've got a clinic to run, but I'll let the nursing staff know what's happened. If you need anything, just press your buzzer, OK?' Lucy showed her how the buzzer worked. 'I'll see you in a bit.'

'Can I have a word, Doctor?' Jack asked as Lucy reached the door.

She summoned every bit of her professional reserve and politeness. 'Yes, of course, Mr Hammond.'

He closed the door behind them and moved so that they were out of Nina's sight. 'Hello, Lucy. It's good to see you again.'

Did he honestly expect her to say the same? She simply remained unsmiling.

His gaze travelled the length of her body and back up to her face. 'You look fantastic.'

What was she supposed to say to that? Was he fishing for a compliment? Probably not. He'd always known his looks turned heads. Again, she remained silent.

'Thanks for what you did for Nina,' he said, trying to take her hand.

She shook him off. 'It's my job, Mr Hammond.'

'Though seeing you again today…it's made me realise what a fool I was,' he said. 'I know I hurt you and I wouldn't have done that for the world. Lord only knows what I was thinking at the time. I must have been mad.'

Yeah, right. There was no answer to that.

'I've never really been able to get you out of my head, you know.'

Lucy shrugged. 'That's not my problem.'

'I suppose what I'm trying to say is…' He tried to slide his arm round her. 'Seeing you again has made me realise how much I've missed you. How much I've wanted you. I'm still in love with you, Lucy.'

Lucy pushed him away. How could she ever, ever have been in love with a man like this? A man so shallow and fickle that he'd let his wife lie in a hospital bed, terrified that she was going to lose yet another baby, while he tried to chat up his ex? 'I don't think so, Jack. Your wife—' she placed extra emphasis on the words '—needs your support right now. The least you can do is give it to her.'

'Lucy…'

She shook her head. 'Whatever was between us, Jack, it was over four years ago. And it's staying that way. Now, excuse me. I have a theatre slot to book for your wife and an antenatal clinic to run.' With relief, she went to the nurses' station and rang Theatre, though her hands were less than steady as she dialled the extension.

Jack was here. After all these years. *Jack.* Jack, the man who'd…

She forced herself to concentrate and booked the slot, then gave Rosemary a quick update and left the ward.

As she walked down the stairs, her vision blurred, and she realised that she was actually crying. She rubbed her eyes hard and stiffened her spine. No way. She'd cried enough tears over Jack Hammond. More like an ocean than a river—and she wasn't going to do it again. Seeing him on her ward had brought it all back, the slicing pain she'd once thought would never end, but she was older and wiser now. She could handle this. She *could*.

By the time she reached the antenatal clinic, she was the cool, calm ice maiden she'd always been at Treverro General. Professional first, last and always. 'Holly about yet?' she asked.

'She called in sick,' Moira, the receptionist, told her. 'Food poisoning.'

Lucy grimaced. 'Poor thing.' She knew how awful food poisoning could be—she'd eaten a dodgy chicken korma once and it had made her ill for three days—but it was going to make life tough for her this morning. She needed a radiographer to help her with an amniocentesis, the procedure where she took a sample of the amniotic fluid surrounding the baby so the lab could culture the baby's skin cells from the fluid to check the chromosomes. 'Is anyone covering for her?' she asked hopefully.

Moira shook her head. 'I did try, the minute I got her message—but everyone else is fully booked up with scans. There are a couple off duty, but I haven't been able to contact them and see if they'd come in for a morning. I could try getting them to do one each with you and delay some of their own scans...'

But the ultrasound clinic always overran, and Lucy had already had some stroppy memos from the finance team about her budget. Not that it was her budget any more, she reminded herself. It was Nic's budget now. *His* problem. Though if she gave him a budgetary headache, she knew he'd carpet her for it. 'Not to worry. I can do it myself,' Lucy said. It just meant that she'd have to concentrate more on the procedure and wouldn't be able to give the parents as much reassurance as she wanted. Though maybe that was what she needed. Something to occupy her mind a hundred and ten per cent.

'Problems?' a voice said behind her.

A voice that only recently had been husky with desire, murmuring, *Lucia mia*.

Nic.

No, she didn't need this added complication right now. She didn't need Nic and she didn't need Jack. She was going to concentrate on her job. Behave yourselves, she told her knees, and spun round to face him. 'Sort of. Holly—one of the radiographers—is ill.'

'And she was working with you this morning on an amnio?' he guessed.

She shrugged. 'I'll manage.'

'I can help if you like,' he offered.

The devil and the deep blue sea, she thought. If she said yes, she'd be able to do her job properly, but she'd also be close to Nic all morning. Nic, who had already cost her more than one sleepless night. She hated this feeling of being out of control, and with Jack around as well to torture her with might-have-beens...

Work, she reminded herself. 'Thanks. Do you want to do the ultrasound or the needle?'

'Ultrasound.' He grinned. 'So *you* get to be the baddie.'

So that was how he was going to play it: light and cool. Just as well. Lucy didn't think she could cope with one of his intense looks. Not when she was all churned up inside as it was. 'OK.' She glanced at her watch. 'Now?'

'I'm all yours, Dr Williams.'

The picture that conjured up meant she didn't trust herself to respond in a similar light-hearted vein, so she ignored him and glanced through the notes for her first patient.

'Mr and Mrs Sanders?' she said to the tearful-looking woman sitting in Waiting Area Two and the silent man by her side.

'Yes.' The woman's voice was hoarse, clearly from crying.

'I'm Lucy Williams, senior registrar, and this is Nic Alberici, the consultant. Would you like to come with us?' She led them through to consulting room with its ultrasound unit.

'You get the special offer today—two for the price of one,' said Nic, 'so there's nothing to worry about.'

'He looks after the monitor and I can concentrate on you,' Lucy added. 'If there's anything you want to ask either of us at any time, just say, but I'll try to tell you exactly what I'm doing and why. Have you had a glass of water while you've been waiting?'

Kay Sanders nodded. 'The midwife said I needed a full bladder.'

'That's so we get a better picture on the screen. If you could lie down on the couch for me, Mrs Sanders, and bare your tummy, Nic will do an ultrasound scan to see how the baby's lying and show me where I can take a little bit of fluid. It won't hurt the baby at all, and the little one shouldn't even notice that I've pinched a bit.'

She smiled warmly at the couple. 'I know it's a horrible situation for you both, but I'll do my best to make this as quick and painless as possible for you. I'm only going to take about ten millilitres of fluid—that's a couple of tea-spoonfuls—and then I'll send it off to the lab for culture. As soon as the results come back, we'll ring you to let you know. If it's bad news, your GP will ring you and ask you to go in to the surgery for a chat.'

'How long will it take?' John Sanders asked.

'Three weeks, I'm afraid. We need the time for the cells to grow,' Nic put in.

Lucy squeezed the woman's hand. Unfortunately, the hospital wasn't yet able to offer the 'fish' test, the chromosomal marker test which only took three days, but maybe Nic could start to influence that. 'This shouldn't hurt, Mrs Sanders—you'll feel a jab as the needle goes in, but I promise it's not as bad as having a tetanus shot.'

'That's one good thing, then.' Kay Sanders was clearly trying to be brave, and Lucy's heart went out to her. The notes showed that the couple had been trying for two years to conceive, and had even been on a waiting list for IVF treatment when they'd discovered that Kay was pregnant. Then the results of a routine screening test had shown that the foetus had a higher-than-average risk of having Down syndrome, so Kay and John had been offered an amniocentesis to clarify the situation.

Lucy put Nic and Jack out of her mind and concentrated on the two worried parents-to-be in front of her.

'The triple test is a screening test, not a definite yes-or-no result. You had higher than normal levels of protein in your blood—what we call alpha-foetal protein or AFP—and your midwife wanted to give you the option of checking the results,' Lucy continued. 'I know it's easy for me to say, but most babies are completely normal, so try not to worry too much.'

Kay nodded, clearly too choked to answer.

'The amniocentesis test carries a very small risk of miscarriage, around one per cent. Our record's actually better than average here as it's less than half a per cent,' Lucy reassured her, 'so we recommend that you take things easy for the next couple of days. I'll give you a leaflet explaining what you can expect to feel—the odd bit of stomach cramp, a bit like period pain, is very common. Though if you get any bleeding or feel any fluid leaking, call your midwife or GP straight away.'

Gently, Nic squeezed gel onto Kay's skin. 'We warm the gel here—not like your midwife in the GP's surgery—and it just helps us get a better picture of the baby.' He passed the ultrasound scanning head over Kay's abdomen, pressing in gently to get the picture Lucy needed.

'If you look on the screen, you'll see your baby,' Lucy said. 'Lying on his or her back with hands behind the head—just like mum. They often do—sometimes I see them crossing their legs and then I look at the mum, who's doing the same thing.'

Nic did some quick measurements. 'According to this, the baby's seventeen weeks.'

'And three days,' John Sanders added.

The triple test results—which showed the risk of spina bifida and Down syndrome—were often wrong if the gestation dates were inaccurate, but that wasn't the situation in this case. Lucy exchanged a glance with Nic and her heart went out to them. 'Well, I can see a nice patch here. I'll be able to keep the needle well away from the baby and he won't even notice. Mrs Sanders, would you mind watching the fish mobile above your head rather than the screen? It's just that it can be upsetting, seeing the needle go in—and if you're upset, the baby will start to fidget. If you could keep as still as possible, it'll be quicker for me to take the fluid.'

'All right.'

The couple were holding hands so tightly, their knuckles showed. 'Now, you'll feel a bit of a scratch.' Gently, Lucy inserted the needle, checking its position against the baby all the time on the ultrasound screen, then drew back the plunger on the syringe to take the fluid. 'All done,' she said, taking the woman's other hand and squeezing it. 'And you were brilliant—you didn't even flinch when I put the needle in. Well done.'

Kay gave her a wobbly smile.

'Have a rest outside for a while while I write up your notes, then if you're feeling OK in twenty minutes or so you can go home—but take it easy and make sure you get plenty of rest for the next day or so. We don't insist on complete bed-rest any more, but you need to be sensible and not overdo things.' She took a leaflet from her clipboard. 'This should answer your questions, but have a read through it while you're sitting in the waiting room. If there's anything you'd like to know that isn't on there, just grab me or one of the midwives and ask us. I know we all look as if we're rushing around, but don't feel you're being a nuisance—you're our patient, too, and we're never too busy to answer questions,' she said, giving the leaflet to Kay. 'If you feel any pain in your abdomen or lose any fluid, or you're worried about anything, ring your midwife straight away. We'll be in touch as soon as the results come back. And, if it helps at all, I can't see any major problems on the scan,' Lucy said.

'Thank you, Doctor,' Kay said gratefully, tears welling in her eyes again.

'And because the test checks the chromosomes of the baby, we can tell you for definite if your baby's a boy or a girl, if you'd like to know,' Lucy added.

Kay nodded. 'I'd like to know, please.'

'OK. I'll make sure it's in your notes. Though we won't be able to tell you that over the phone—we'll send you a letter to confirm it.'

The couple left the room. When Lucy had finished labelling the sample, Nic smiled at her. 'You've got a great way with patients, Lucy. You took them through it clearly without being patronising, and you put the mother at her ease.'

'As would any senior registrar worth his or her salt,' Lucy reminded him. 'They're in a horrible situation and it's my job to make it as easy for them as possible. If I can't do it by now, I shouldn't be in this job.'

And until last week, she *hadn't* been in this job—she'd been doing his job.

Nic held both hands up. 'Hey, I wasn't trying to patronise you.'

'Of course not.'

He smiled ruefully. 'We make a great team. We work on the same wavelength and I like that—I don't want to fight with you, Lucia *mia*.'

'Would you please stop calling me that?' she hissed. 'I'm not *your* Lucy.'

He didn't say anything. He didn't have to. His eyes said it all for him: *yet*. He brushed the backs of his fingers against his cheek and she shivered as if he'd touched *her*. 'It's a shame you didn't come out with me on our day off.'

Why had he had to say 'our'? Linking them together like that? They weren't an item. Not even *close*.

'I went for a long walk on the beach down the road, and tried a traditional Cornish pasty.' He gave her a sidelong look, one he'd probably calculated to melt her, she thought crossly. 'But it would have been even better if you'd been there to share it with me.'

'I'm sure you'd have plenty of offers of company if you asked.' Just like Jack had.

'I don't want just any company.' He rubbed the pad of his thumb against his lower lip and her knees buckled. Nic wasn't playing fair. OK, he'd kept his promise and he wasn't touching her—but she could imagine how it would feel if his fingers were touching her skin instead of his own. Worse, she *knew* what it felt like, and she wanted more.

Or was it just because she'd seen Jack again?

'I only want you,' Nic murmured, holding her gaze.

It would be so, so easy to say yes.

And then she'd spend a lifetime regretting it. Happy-ever-after didn't exist. She knew that. The proof of the pudding was sitting right upstairs, next to his wife.

She backed away and crossed her arms defensively. 'I've already told you, I'm not looking for a relationship.'

'You kissed me back at the ball, Lucia *mia*,' he reminded her softly.

She coughed. 'Everyone's entitled to their mistakes.'

'It wasn't a mistake.'

'Let's agree to differ. We have patients to see and a budget to stick to.'

He stared at her for a long, long moment, then nodded. 'As you wish.'

He kept out of her way for the rest of the clinic. Lucy wasn't sure whether to be relieved or disappointed. She'd half expected him to suggest having lunch together, and then she saw him talking to Beth, one of the midwives. He was smiling at her—the special smile Lucy had begun to think was reserved for *her*—and Beth was smiling back just as warmly.

Worse, they left the clinic together. It hadn't take Nic long to choose a replacement for her company—so much for his 'I only want you'.

Don't be such a dog in the manger, Lucy told herself. You don't want Nic. You've already told him as much. Don't begrudge Beth her chance of happiness.

Though she knew she was lying to herself. She *did* want Nic, and she was as jealous as hell of the young midwife. Which was precisely why she should stay well away from Nic Alberici. Just like her mother and her sisters, she had appalling judgement in men. And she wasn't ever going to let herself get hurt like that again. She'd already been there, done that and worn the T-shirt with Jack. And she was a fast learner. She didn't repeat her mistakes.

Ever.

CHAPTER FIVE

TRYING to ignore the twinge of misery in her heart, Lucy gathered her notes together and went to see her next patient. The woman sitting in the consulting room, supported by a nurse, was clutching a cardboard bowl and her face was very pale.

'Hello, Mrs Jacobs. I'm Lucy Williams, senior registrar.'

'Hello.' The woman's face tightened and she closed her eyes, as if willing herself not to be sick.

'You're sixteen weeks now?' Lucy asked gently, glancing at her notes.

She nodded.

'And you've been feeling like this since six weeks?'

'Yeah. This one's definitely going to be an only child,' Sonia Jacobs said, grimacing.

'Are you keeping much down?'

She shook her head. 'Hardly anything. I'm sick from the minute I get up to the minute I go to bed—and half the night, too. I've tried ginger and sniffing lemons and acupressure bands—nothing works.'

'Would you mind if I examined you?' Lucy asked.

Slowly, Sonia got up on the couch, and was promptly sick. Lucy immediately dampened a paper towel and handed it to her, together with a box of tissues.

'Sorry,' Sonia said, almost crying.

'Not to worry. We'll have you feeling better soon,' Lucy said comfortingly. Gently, she examined Sonia's abdomen. Her skin wasn't as elastic as it should have been and didn't spring back immediately when it was pinched: one of the first symptoms of dehydration. Given that Sonia was feeling sick all the time as well as being sick, she probably wasn't eating or drinking much in the first place.

'Some mums are unlucky with morning sickness—it lasts all day and seems to go on for ever,' Lucy said. 'It's what we call hyperemesis gravidarum—basically, it means you're vomiting a lot during pregnancy. Though I don't like prescribing anti-nausea drugs.' Not after the thalidomide problem—even though it had been decades before, doctors were still wary. 'I'm worried that you're not getting enough nutrients and you're a little dehydrated. I'd like to admit you for a couple of days to give you some fluids.'

'Can't I just try to drink a bit more at home?' Sonia asked.

'If you're not keeping anything down, you'll just be making life harder for yourself,' Lucy said. 'We'll put you on a drip—that is, we'll put a very fine needle in your hand and pass some fluids through it. It won't make you sick and you'll feel a lot better,' she said. 'Don't worry, the baby will be fine,' she added. 'Research shows that when your baby's growing well, you're more likely to suffer morning sickness.' She grinned. 'Though I think when your baby arrives, he's going to be a hungry one who'll scoff all day! Now, if you'd like to go home and pack whatever you need, I'll arrange for you to be admitted to the ward this afternoon. I'll be up to see you on my rounds, and we'll see how you're getting on in a couple of days—when you're feeling better and keeping a bit more down, you'll be able to go home again.'

Sonia nodded. 'Can my husband come in and visit me?'

'Of course,' Lucy said. 'And if you're worried about anything, just ask one of the midwives—they're a really nice bunch on River.'

'Thank you, Doctor,' Sonia said.

'I'll see you later on,' Lucy said with a smile.

She couldn't quite face lunch—the idea of seeing Nic and Beth together in the canteen was too much for her—so she headed back for the ward. Her Theatre slot had been put back by an emergency, so she got her paperwork out of the way.

She was just going to check on Nina when Jack came out of the side room.

'I've been waiting for you,' he said.

'Is Nina all right?' she asked, immediately assuming the worst.

'Yeah.' He shrugged. 'I'd have called one of the midwives if there was a problem. That's what you said, wasn't it?'

'Yes.'

'No, it's you I was looking for,' he said softly. 'Lucy. I've called myself all kinds of fools. I never should have let you go.'

'It's all water under the bridge,' she said crisply.

'It doesn't have to be.'

Did he really think she was the type to have an affair with a married man? Particularly one who'd already brought her world crashing down once? Did she have GULLIBLE tattooed on her forehead or something? 'Yes, it does. It's over, Jack.'

'Is it? Can you honestly say with your hand on your heart that you never think about me? That you don't miss what we had?'

'Yes.'

'Look me in the eye and say it.'

Her lip curled. 'I don't have to do anything, Jack. I certainly don't have to justify myself to you. Now, leave me alone.'

'It's not over, Lucy. It never really was. You and me.

We were good together; don't you remember? That day at the waterfall, when we—'

'Was a long time ago,' Lucy cut in. She definitely didn't want to think about that day. The day when she and Jack had made love for the first time. When she'd realised how much she'd loved him. 'It's in the past and it's staying that way. If Nina doesn't need me, other patients do.'

He caught her hand. 'But *I* need you, Lucy. I can't stop thinking about you. The way we used to be together. The way you felt against me.' He gave her a lazy smile and rubbed his thumb against her palm. 'The way we used to spend whole days in bed together. Do you remember? We'd only get up for long enough to make toast—and then we'd end up having to chuck it away because it got cold, because we hadn't been able to wait long enough for it to cook before making love again.' He lifted his other hand to stroke her face. 'It was so good between us.'

So why did you end it the way you did? Lucy asked silently. Why did you hurt me so badly?

'Meet me later,' he said. 'Tonight. We'll go for a meal, talk a bit. And maybe then…' He cupped her face, catching her off guard, and lowered his mouth to hers.

For one heart-stopping second, Lucy almost responded to the familiar pressure of his lips—and then she remembered where they were. And who was in the room just behind them. She shoved hard at his chest. 'Get off me!'

'You don't mean that. Come on, Lucy,' Jack wheedled. 'You know you feel the same way I do.'

'Is this man bothering you, Dr Williams?' an icy voice demanded.

'It's fine. I'm handling the situation,' Lucy said.

'If you're sure you don't need any help,' Nic said, giving Jack a ferocious stare.

Jack shrugged it off. 'Lucy and I go back a long, long way.'

'Then you should know that when she says no, she means it,' Nic informed him tartly. 'And there are rules in this hospital about abusing staff. If I catch you annoying one of my staff again—and Lucy in particular—I'll throw you out personally and warn Security that you're barred from the hospital. Understand?'

'You and whose army?' Jack sneered.

'Just me. And that's more than enough for your sort, believe me,' Nic said, his voice very quiet and very, very dangerous. 'Dr Williams—I need to discuss a case with you in my office. Now would be a good time.'

'Of course, Mr Alberici.' Lucy refused to look at Jack again and accompanied Nic to his office in silence.

'Take a seat,' Nic said, closing the door behind him.

Lucy did so.

'Care to tell me what all that was about?'

'Nothing important,' she said, lifting her chin. 'What's this case you wanted to discuss?'

'There wasn't one. I just thought you could do with an excuse to leave the ward. Fast.'

'Don't worry, I can handle the situation.'

'Lucy, I don't doubt your ability with patients,' Nic said, 'but it looked as if the guy was hassling you. Which makes it my problem, and *I'll* handle it, as your boss.'

She narrowed her eyes. 'Yeah, right. Pull rank, why don't you?'

He raked a hand through his hair. 'Lucy, you're as capable as I am of running this ward. You did it for weeks before I got the job. I know that and I'm trying to stay out of your hair and not interfere with the way you're doing your job.'

'What's wrong with the way I'm doing my job?' she demanded.

'Nothing!' He rolled his eyes. 'OK. Tell me this. If a patient or relative was hassling one of your staff, what would you do?'

'Step in, defuse the situation, make sure everyone knew the rules and that I'd enforce them if I had to,' she said.

'Precisely. And that's what I'm doing now. I'm doing exactly what you'd do in my shoes. So don't give me a hard time about it, OK?'

She flushed. 'I'm sorry. I suppose it must be as tough for you, having a second in command who was in charge until you came along.'

'So we'll make the best of it. Together. As a team.' Nic's voice softened. 'Are you all right, Lucy?'

'I'm fine,' she said through gritted teeth.

'You don't look it. He's upset you—you're shaking.'

'I'm not.' She whipped her hands behind her back before he could challenge her to prove it.

He smiled at her. 'Come on, I'll shout you a coffee at Pat's Place.'

'I said I'm *fine*, Nic.'

He looked as if he didn't believe her, but at least he didn't argue with her. 'I know you've got a slot in Theatre this afternoon, so you're due a break before you operate—coincidentally enough, I'm due a break right now, too. So let's get out of here before someone bleeps us.'

Lucy was about to snarl at him to leave her alone, but stopped herself. It wasn't Nic's fault that Jack had turned up—or that Jack had behaved the way he had. Jack the lad. Jack the selfish bastard, only thinking of himself and what he wanted. Jack, who actually thought she'd fall into his arms again. Jack, who'd had the nerve to remind her of the time they'd first made love, of the time they'd lived together... Jack, who'd never given her a real explanation for what he'd done, let alone a proper apology.

Though 'sorry' wouldn't be nearly enough.

Nic didn't press her for more details on their way to the café, but the silence between them wasn't awkward either. He was just giving her some much-needed space, and Lucy appreciated it. Right now, she could do with being several hundred miles away from Treverro. Preferably on some remote Scottish island where she'd be guaranteed never to see Jack Hammond again.

'If you find us a table, I'll get the coffees,' he said as they walked into the café. 'And before you insist on paying your share, Dr Independent Williams, you can buy me cake and coffee next time I have the day from hell. Deal?'

'Deal.' Though she didn't think that Nic would have this sort of day. Not ever. She hadn't expected it in a million years, being called to treat Jack's wife. She really, really should have walked out and let someone else deal with it. Yet Nina had looked so frightened, so desperate. How could Lucy, as a doctor, have refused to help the poor woman?

Nic put a mug of mochaccino and a muffin in front of her. 'Pat's trying a new recipe—toffee *crème* and pecan,' he said.

'Thanks.' Lucy took a swig of coffee. And the muffin was exactly what she needed—sweet, stodgy comfort food.

Nic waited until she'd finished before he spoke again. 'Better?' he asked.

'Yeah.' She forced a smile to her face. 'Thanks. I needed a breather.'

'So what's the story?'

A story she didn't want to talk about. To *think* about, even. She wanted to keep it buried so she never had to feel that kind of misery and disillusion again. 'There is no story.'

'Talk to me, Lucy,' he said softly. 'You'll feel better than if you keep it all locked up inside.'

'I wouldn't even know where to start.'

'Try the beginning.'

She sighed. 'OK. Though I trust you'll respect my confidence. No one here at Treverro knows about this.'

Nic's heart missed a beat. Lucy was going to trust him with something no one else knew? 'Of course. Lucy, I know what hospital grapevines are like. I won't breathe a word to anyone else.'

'It's my cerclage patient—Nina Hammond.'

He waited. If he asked a question now, he might push her back behind her defensive wall. He had to let her tell him in her own time.

'She's married to my ex. Jack. The one you saw…' She took a deep, shuddering breath and the look of pain on her face made Nic want to push Jack Hammond through a window.

'It was a bit of a messy break-up. Once I'd picked up the pieces, I left London and came here.'

To Cornwall. As far away from her ex as possible. Whatever had happened between them must have been really bad—from what he'd seen of Lucy, he didn't think she was the type to run away. It would have been easy for her to resign from her job here once he'd taken over—but she hadn't. She'd stayed to see it through. Lucy Williams was a fighter, not a coward.

'I never thought I'd see him again.' She shrugged. 'But Cornwall's a really popular holiday spot, so I should have anticipated running into him around here at some point. I just didn't expect it to be here, at work.'

'Do you want me to look after the Hammonds?' he asked.

She shook her head. 'It's OK. I'll manage.'

'Lucy, it's not a good idea. Apart from the fact that he's hassling you now, you know the patient so you're involved.'

Lucy shook her head. 'Actually, no. Nina and I never knew each other.'

'So he met her after you broke up?'

She smiled bitterly. 'You know, I didn't think Jack could sink any lower in my estimation. But the fact that he came on to me just now—while his wife was lying in my ward, terrified that she was going to lose her baby—how could I *ever* have got involved with someone like that? How could I have misjudged his character so badly?'

Nic's fists tightened and he made himself relax them deliberately. Being macho wasn't going to help Lucy. Right now, she needed understanding, not puffed-up male bravado. 'Hey, it's not your fault the guy turned out to be a low-life.'

'No?' Lucy made a face. 'I'm like the rest of my family. I've got rotten judgement when it comes to my life partner. We're all useless at this kind of thing.'

'Everyone makes mistakes, Lucy. Don't blame yourself.' He squeezed her hand. 'Look, if it'll make things easier for you, I'm happy to swap a case with you.'

She shook her head. 'Even if I don't do the cerclage on Nina, I know Jack'll seek me out again. I've told him I'm not interested, but once Jack gets an idea into his head… Let's just say he's persistent.'

'Oh, Lucy.' Sitting there, holding her hand, had probably blown his common sense into some far universe—it was the only explanation Nic could think of for the words that came out of his mouth next. 'There's one thing you could do to prove to him you're not interested.'

'What?'

'Show him you're off limits—you're someone else's girl.'

Lucy blinked hard. 'Someone else's girl?'

'If he knows you're still single, he'll think you're pining for him. Whereas if he sees you with someone…he'll know you're not. And then he'll leave you alone.'

She was silent for a long, long time, clearly thinking about Nic's suggestion. The volcano was about to explode at any minute, Nic thought. She was going to slap his face, throw the remains of his coffee over him, storm out.

Instead, she nodded. 'Good point.'

She was going to go ahead with it?

'So what's the plan?'

The plan? Nic didn't have one! He had to improvise—fast. 'We go back onto the ward. You go up to Theatre. I tell him he has to wait for his wife in the dayroom or in her room. He sees you arriving at the door after the operation—and he overhears you make a date with the man in your life.' This was the crunch. The bit where she'd say no. 'Me.'

'And you think it'd work?'

Yes! Yes! his heart screamed. 'It's worth a try,' he said, as casually as he could.

There was a long, long pause and Nic could feel his blood pressure rising. Was she going to knock him back?

'OK,' she said at last.

She'd agreed? Nic surreptitiously pinched himself. Yes, he was awake. 'Fine. I'd better get going. Bleep me when you get out of Theatre, and we'll put Plan A into action,' he said softly.

*   *   *

It was a crazy plan, Lucy thought, but she wanted Jack out of her life. Now and for ever. And Nic had a point: the only way Jack would leave her alone was if he thought she was involved with someone else.

No, not just someone else. *Nic*. Involved with Nic.

The idea terrified her and excited her at the same time. But it was just a smokescreen, she reminded herself. This wasn't the same as actually having a relationship with Nic. She wasn't his girlfriend, his lover—she wasn't *anyone's* girlfriend or lover. She was her own person, and she had a fulfilling career to concentrate on.

Even so, she was glad she had the operation to deal with so she had to give her full attention to her work, and even gladder that Mal was assisting. Her SHO hadn't seen a cerclage done before and it was a good opportunity to teach him; plus, she'd have to keep herself well under control in front of him. She couldn't risk him teasing her about all this.

In Theatre, Mal dropped his habitual clowning and assisted her well, asking intelligent questions—showing the side of him she liked best. Absorbed in her work, Lucy almost forgot about the turmoil in her life. But as soon as she'd finished the suturing, cleaned up and asked Mal to check on another patient, it came back to her with full force. She was going to have to face Jack again. And show him that she wasn't interested in him—now or ever.

She bleeped Nic, and he was waiting for her outside Nina Hammond's door when she came down to the ward.

'How did it go?' he asked.

'Fine. As long as she takes it easy…' Lucy shrugged. 'She's going to need a lot of support. Support I don't think Jack's going to give her.' No doubt when Nina had had her miscarriages, he'd been playing the field, dropping her off at hospital, letting the nurses look after her and going straight to the nearest club to exercise his pulling power.

'Talking of Jack, he's watching us,' Nic said very softly. 'As far as he's concerned, we're just two colleagues discussing a case. We need to prove you're off limits.'

'How?'

'Kiss me.'

'What?'

'Or let me kiss you. Like this.' He bent his head and touched his lips to hers. What started out as a gentle kiss suddenly turned explosive, and Lucy was kissing him back with abandon, caressing his face and revelling in the beginnings of stubble rubbing against her fingers.

A loud cough brought them both back to reality.

'How's my wife?' Jack demanded. The suppressed fury in his face told Lucy that Nic's idea had worked—and how!

'Everything was very straightforward, no complications. She should be fine,' Lucy said.

'Though we'll keep her on bed-rest here for the next twenty-four hours,' Nic said. 'I'm sorry that it's going to interrupt your holiday, but it's standard procedure and I'd prefer to err on the side of caution, especially as your wife's had several miscarriages already.' He held out his hand. 'I'm sorry, I didn't introduce myself earlier. Niccolo Alberici, obstetric consultant.'

Jack took his hand as if it was something the cat had dragged in. 'Jack Hammond.'

Nic slid his arm round Lucy's shoulders. 'I apologise if we embarrassed you just now, Mr Hammond. We try not to let our private life spill over into work, which is why I didn't explain to you earlier that Lucy's more than just a member of my staff. But when it comes to *amore*…' He smiled. 'When you're in love, sometimes you can't help yourself, don't you find?'

Jack shuffled on the spot, looking uncomfortable. Lucy just bet he was wondering how much she'd told Nic about him. Well, she wasn't going to enlighten him. Let him sweat a bit, for a change.

'I'm sure you must have questions for Lucy, so I'll leave you to it.' Nic dropped a kiss on top of Lucy's head, still playing his part to perfection. 'Bleep me when you're ready to go home, Lucia *mia*.'

It was working! Lucy thought gleefully. The disgruntlement on Jack's face was plain. 'Remember it's your turn to cook tonight, darling,' she said.

'Again? You're a tough woman,' Nic grumbled jokingly, winked and left them to it.

'So—you're seeing that smarmy Italian?' Jack asked when Nic was out of earshot.

'That's my business. And Nic isn't the slightest bit smarmy.' Which was true. He was infuriating, a flirt, drove her crazy...but never smarmy.

'But—' Jack began.

Lucy gave him a scornful look. 'What did you expect? That I'd eat my heart out over you and wait for you to change your mind again?'

Jack flushed dully.

'Now, do you have any questions about Nina's care?'

'I— No, I suppose not.'

'She's going to need you, Jack. She's going to feel as if everything's her fault. So your job's to reassure her and support her and tell her how much you love her. OK?'

'Yeah,' he muttered.

'Good. I'll probably see you *both* tomorrow, then.' She gave him a tight smile, gathered up her clipboard and a set of notes and swept off to see her next patient.

CHAPTER SIX

'YOU'RE a dark horse, Luce,' Malcolm said, grinning. 'How long have you and His Lordship been...you know?' He nudged her.

'I haven't the faintest idea what you're talking about, Malcolm,' Lucy said coolly, hoping that her SHO hadn't noticed the tremor running through her.

'Oh, come on! Beth saw the pair of you kissing outside one of the side rooms a few minutes ago. Quite a clinch, she said. A snog, not just a little peck on the cheek. And you both sneak off together on a regular basis. *Now* we know why,' he teased.

'We do not "sneak off", as you put it. We merely adjourn to Pat's Place. Where we discuss work in a civilised way,' Lucy said.

'You don't discuss work with *me* like that,' he retorted.

She ruffled his hair. 'Malcy, dearest, if you were a civilised human being, instead of being like my kid brothers at their most annoying, I'd have patient conferences over coffee with you, too. You did well in Theatre today. If you're a good boy tomorrow and keep it up, I might even buy you a mochaccino at Pat's.' She blew him a kiss and walked away, though inside she was shaking.

Why hadn't she seen this coming? Why had she agreed to Nic's stupid plan? Why hadn't she just swapped the Hammonds for one of his cases? Why?

She asked herself the same question several times in the next half-hour, when the midwives started quizzing her, too.

'So does our Italian sex god kiss as beautifully as he looks?' Beth asked.

'How should I know?' Lucy responded.

'Come on, Lucy. I *saw* you in the corridor. It was enough to steam up my glasses!'

'It's not what you think,' Lucy said, feeling her face grow hot. 'It's complicated.'

'You're a lucky cow, Lucy Williams. He's *gorgeous*.'

'Beth, I…' She sighed. 'He's my boss.'

'Who cares? He's the sexiest man ever to have walked into this hospital,' Beth said cheerfully. 'But at least now I know why he was polite but firm when I asked him out the other day.'

'You asked him out?' Lucy was shocked.

'I didn't know you were interested in him—I just thought he was young, free, single and gorgeous. But he turned me down, obviously because he had someone else in his sights. You.' Beth gave her a broad wink. 'Go for it, girl!'

Rosemary was even worse. 'Talk about the lady doth protest too much, Lucy Williams. Now we know your little secret!' she said.

Secret? Did she mean Lucy's supposed affair with Nic— or did she know all about Jack Hammond? No, she couldn't. Nobody knew the truth about Jack. Not the whole truth. Not even Nic.

'Don't look so worried,' Rosemary said with a grin. 'It couldn't happen to a nicer couple.'

'We are *not* a couple,' Lucy said through gritted teeth.

'Come off it. Look at the way you work together— you're a perfect double act on the ward. I've never seen such teamwork. You clicked right from the start, and I wondered how long it'd take you to get together in private as well as professionally.'

'There's nothing to talk about,' Lucy insisted.

'Oh, look! There goes another flying pig,' Rosemary teased, pointing to the ceiling.

Lucy realised her misery must have shown on her face, because Rosemary gave her a hug. 'Hey, I'm only teasing. Half of us are jealous because he's so gorgeous, and all of us think it's about time you stopped working so hard and had some fun.'

By the time her shift ended, Lucy was extremely glad to remove her white coat and hang it in her locker. But she didn't even make it out of the department. Nic was there in the corridor. Waiting for her, by the looks of it.

'You OK?' he asked.

'Fine,' she said, tight-lipped.

'Jack Hammond hasn't tried it on with you again?'

'No, he's left me alone. Unfortunately, I can't say the same about the hospital rumour machine.'

'Ah.' Nic had the grace to look penitent. 'I didn't think of that.'

'Neither did I.'—

'The way I see it, you've got three choices. Number one, tell them the truth.'

Her eyes widened. The truth? She hadn't even told Nic the full story! And if she did, she'd have to face a repeat of all the pitying looks she'd had in London... 'No way.'

'Number two, ignore them. It'll blow over.'

Eventually. He was right there. 'And number three?'

He took her hand, kissed her palm and curled her fingers over the imprint of his kiss. 'Not telling, Lucia *mia*. You'll slap my face.'

'Nic,' she said warningly.

'OK.' He launched into a stream of Italian.

'Funny guy,' she snarled.

'Come on. Let's get out of here.' He opened the door

and shepherded her out of the department. 'You've had the day from hell and right now you need a bit of TLC.'

'I'm perfectly fine,' Lucy said frostily.

He didn't argue with her, just smiled. 'You're going to pass on my bruschetta, then?'

'What bruschetta?'

'You told me it was my turn to cook tonight, did you not?'

'That was just to make Jack think I...' Her throat dried.

'And it's a great idea. I'll cook you dinner. As your *friend*,' he emphasised. 'Coming?'

'What about my bicycle?'

'It's secured, yes?' At her nod, he said, 'Pick it up later. And if you're worrying about people seeing us leaving together, it won't make a difference because they're already talking about us. Tomorrow morning, something else will have knocked you off the top gossip spot, and everything will go back to normal.'

Normal? Right then, Lucy wasn't sure that anything would ever be normal again.

'I'm hungry,' he said. 'And if you really, really hate my cooking then I have ice cream in the freezer. Luxury ice cream.' He grinned. 'And that's an offer you can't possibly refuse.'

Nic gave her a sidelong look as he held the passenger door of his car open for her. He'd seen her expression as she'd looked at his car—it was obvious she'd expected him to drive some macho sports car. 'Disappointed?'

'What?'

'That I drive a boring, mid-range Audi rather than a Ferrari?'

Lucy flushed. 'I'm trying not to stereotype you.'

Oh, wasn't she? 'Good. Because I never wanted a red

Italian sports car.' He chuckled. 'I wanted an Italian motorbike. A big, fast one. I bought a Ducati.'

'So why the switch to the car?'

'My mother.' He climbed into the driver's seat. 'Her reaction was more Italian than my dad's when I came home with it. She yelled at me—in Italian—that I was going to kill myself and would I be so pleased with myself then, and she slammed every single door in the house, hard enough to knock a couple of pictures off the wall and break the glass in them. We didn't speak for three days, and then I did a stint in A and E. We lost a twenty-year-old who'd come off his bike—a much smaller bike than mine—and I had to break the news to his parents. I realised then I couldn't ever put my mother through the hell of learning her only son had died in an accident, and I sold the Duc the next morning.'

'And now you're Mr Predictable?'

'Oh, I wouldn't say *that*,' he told her, his voice soft and low. She flushed spectacularly, and he chuckled. 'Don't play with fire, Lucia *mia*. My self-control's good—but not that good.'

Neither was hers, she thought. This was a stupid idea, going home with Nic. Seeing Jack again had brought back all her old insecurities. If Nic paid her the slightest attention, she'd probably fall straight into his arms, be another notch on his bedpost and then have to cope with seeing him go after his next conquest. Hadn't he already admitted that he couldn't resist a challenge? And what more of a challenge could he have than the hospital's ice maiden?

She was silent as Nic drove them back to his flat, a conversion in the old priory at the edge of Treverro. 'Wow,' Lucy said as he ushered her inside and dropped his suit jacket over the back of a sofa. The Gothic-arched windows let light flood into the rooms, and everything screamed expensive luxury—white walls, honey-coloured wide wooden floorboards, a thick cream wool rug before a honey-coloured marble fire surround, dark gold sofas with huge plump cushions and matching curtains. Bookshelves ran along one wall, filled with well-thumbed medical textbooks and an array of paperbacks.

'I can't take credit for the décor. It's rented, though I might try persuading the owner to sell it to me,' Nic said. 'I did think about commuting from Plymouth every day, but I really didn't want an hour's drive each way as well as a full day at work.' He gestured to the windows. 'These almost make up for losing a view over Plymouth Sound.'

He had a place on the waterfront in Plymouth? They cost an arm and a leg. Maybe Nic had grown up rich—it suddenly struck her how little she knew about him. Just that his father was Italian, his mother was English, he had two older sisters and he'd once owned a very fast Italian motorbike.

The idea of Nic wearing leathers made a hundred butterflies start doing the salsa in her stomach. He'd look stunning. Black leather trousers, a loose black T-shirt, black leather boots, a fitted black leather jacket left casually undone. And carrying a single white rose as he sang a serenade outside her bedroom window…

She gasped. Where on earth had *that* come from?

He'd obviously heard her gasp or seen the panic in her face, because he smiled at her. 'Relax, Lucy. We both know the rules. I won't lay a finger on you without your permission.' He loosened his tie. 'Glass of wine?'

'I shouldn't. I'll be cycling later.'

'You don't have to.'

He was expecting her to spend the night with him? Her eyes widened in shock.

'I'll call you a taxi,' he said, beckoning to her. 'Come and talk to me while I'm cooking.'

So he *wasn't* expecting her just to fall into his bed. Lucy wasn't sure whether to be relieved or disappointed.

'The kitchen's this way.'

The kitchen was narrow, galley-style, but again it screamed luxury, all beech—real wood, not just veneer—and black granite. Most of the appliances were hidden away behind beech doors, but Lucy guessed that they'd be the same top brand as the cooker and hob.

'Red or white?' Nic asked as he took two plain narrow-stemmed glasses from a cupboard.

'What are you cooking?'

'Hmm… Do you like chicken?'

'Yes.'

'Then I'll cook chicken *cacciatore*,' he decided. 'So we should have white. Italian, of course.' He took a bottle from the built-in rack hidden at the side of a unit, opened it deftly and poured them both a glass of Soave. 'And Italian music. Well, French—sung by an Italian.' He had a micro-system hidden in an alcove; he flicked a switch and the kitchen was flooded with classical music.

She didn't recognise the haunting lament. Instead of being backed by a full orchestra, the tenor was backed simply by a classical guitar. 'This is lovely. What is it?'

'"*Elle est là*", from Bizet's *La Jolie Fille de Perth*,' he told her. 'I heard this piece on the radio once and it haunted me for days—in the end, I went into this little classical specialist shop in Plymouth and hummed it to the guy behind the counter. He recognised it and ordered it for me.'

Could Nic sing like this? she wondered, then was cross with herself. It wasn't a given that all Italian or Welsh men could sing like angels. He'd already told her not to stereotype him. And she really had to rid herself of that vision of him as the man in black, serenading her by moonlight. 'Anything I can do to help?' she asked.

'No. Just stay and chat to me. Or have a wander round the flat, if you like.'

It was tempting—a chance to learn more about Nic, his tastes in music and books and films. But right now she wanted to be with him. Watch him as he worked. As he cooked for her.

Her man.

Except he wasn't *really* hers. It was just a smokescreen they'd concocted so Jack would leave her alone.

Lucy leaned back against a worktop, sipped her wine and watched him as he deftly prepared first the bruschetta— ciabatta bread brushed with garlic, topped with dolcelatte, mushrooms, pancetta, off-the-vine tomatoes and a drizzle of olive oil—then whizzed up a sauce of white wine, tomatoes, onions and olives, throwing in extra garlic and a handful of mushrooms. And fresh herbs, she noted, from one of the little pots on his window-sill.

'I told you before, I enjoy cooking,' he said as he saw her glance. 'And I only use first-class ingredients. Fresh, rather than dried. Before you ask, yes, I do make my own pasta. I learned how in Tuscany, no less, from my *nonna*— my Italian grandmother.' He grinned. 'You'd like Nonna. She's like you—very direct, no nonsense. And she likes to have things her own way.'

Lucy was about to protest when she realised that he was teasing her. Flirting with her. It threw her off balance and she took refuge in her wine.

He prepared the chicken as the bruschetta was cooking, threw some vegetables in a steamer and two large potatoes in the microwave, then slid the bruschetta onto two plates and left the chicken simmering in the sauce. 'Bring the wine and our glasses,' he told her, gathering up the plates.

Lucy followed him to the small dining table set in an alcove with a view of the moors. 'You're overlooking the sunset,' she said.

'And I get the sunrise in my bedroom,' he told her. 'It's one of the things I like most about the flat. The light's perfect.'

Nic's bedroom. Excitement rippled at the base of her spine and she suppressed it ruthlessly. No. She wasn't going to start putting Nic and bed in the same thought. Too dangerous. 'The bruschetta's very good,' she said, changing the subject.

'Relax, Lucy,' he said softly, almost as if he'd read her mind. 'I've already told you I'm not going to do anything you don't want me to do, and I'm a man of my word. You're here as my friend, my colleague. I respect you.'

There was a lump in her throat the size of a rock. She didn't want Nic Alberici to be *kind* to her, like a stray puppy. But she was too scared to take their relationship in the direction he'd told her he wanted it to take.

She shouldn't have come here. She really, really shouldn't have come here. Especially with Jack in the background, reminding her what a disaster she was when it came to relationships. She didn't want a three-date affair. But she wasn't ready for a rest-of-our-lives moment either. Right now, she didn't know what she *did* want.

Except for Nic to kiss her.

Which she knew would be a very, very bad idea.

Miserably, she forced herself to eat the rest of her bruschetta. Nic topped up her glass.

'I'm cycling home,' she reminded him.

'No, you're not. I'm sending you home in a taxi. Your bike'll be fine at the hospital overnight,' he said. 'You've had a rough day, and you need to relax.'

But how could she, when she was so aware of his nearness? So aware of the possibilities? So aware of his beautiful mouth?

He saved her from having to make polite conversation by disappearing back into the kitchen and returning with their laden plates.

'This is very good,' she said after the first mouthful.

'Thank you. My father's hopeless in the kitchen and my mother was determined I wouldn't grow up the same—and when Dad told me being able to cook would put me in a better negotiating position to get me out of doing the washing-up, I leapt at the chance to learn.'

As he chatted on, keeping the subject light and harmless, Lucy found her tension easing. By the time they'd finished eating, she was surprised to realise she was actually enjoying herself.

'As you cooked, I should do the washing-up,' she said.

'No need. I have a dishwasher,' he said with a grin. And then his face grew serious. 'But you can do two things for me.'

'What's that?'

'Firstly, loosen your hair.' He swallowed hard. 'Lucy…I promised you I wouldn't touch you without your permission, and I keep my promises. But right now, what I want to do most in the world is to run my hands through your hair.'

'My hair?'

'Mmm-hmm. The way you wear it at work drives me crazy. I've been trying to imagine what it would be like all loose over your shoulders. It looks like sunlight. And I want to know whether it feels as soft and warm as I've been fantasising. Whether it smells like sunlight.'

His words sent a shiver through her. But they were just words, she reminded himself. He was Italian. Had a silver tongue. Could talk anyone round to his way of thinking. 'It's just hair, Nic.'

'It's beautiful,' he said simply. 'Like your mouth. And, believe me, your mouth's given me a lot of difficult moments lately.'

She flushed. He could have been talking for her, too. 'Nic…'

'I know, I know. I'm not supposed to be saying this sort of thing to you. I have all these good intentions,' he said ruefully, 'but they just melt whenever you're near me. I'm OK when I'm with a patient—but the second I'm not, all I can think about is you.'

That made two of them.

His voice deepened slightly, taking on a note of raw desire. 'You, and how much I want to touch you, how much I want to kiss you. Right now, it would be so easy to take your hand and kiss my way up to your shoulder. To touch my mouth to your pulse point. To hold you close to me. To tangle my hands in your hair and kiss you until neither of us can see straight.'

She wasn't sure which of them moved. Maybe both of them. But then she was in his arms and he was kissing her, his mouth dropping tiny butterfly kisses along her eyelids, her cheekbones, the line of her jaw, purposely teasing her mouth until she slid her hands behind his neck and pulled his mouth onto hers.

Nic's kisses were so different from Jack's. Asking, not demanding. Sweet. Seductive. Promising. Offering.

He teased her at first, keeping to those same tiny butterfly kisses, tracing the outline of her lips until she slid the tip of her tongue between his lips. And then he kissed her with abandon, his hands tangled in her hair, and she matched him kiss for kiss, hunger for hunger.

When he broke the kiss, they were both shaking. His

eyes were very, very dark, the pupils expanded with desire, and his mouth was reddened and slightly swollen. Lucy knew she must look the same, because her mouth was tingling. Worse, she wanted to do it all over again—but this time with fewer barriers between them.

'Lucia *mia*.' He took his hand and placed it over his heart, against the soft, warm silk of his shirt. 'Feel what you do to me.'

The same as what he did to her: his heart was beating so hard, so fast, she could feel it thudding against her palm. This was dangerous. Too dangerous. She pulled her hand back and moved out of reach. 'This isn't fair, Nic.'

'I know, and I'm sorry. I just...' He groaned. 'I don't know how to explain it. You've knocked me for six.'

Said the man who'd taken a different woman to lunch every day since he'd joined the hospital. Probably dinner, too. 'I bet you say that to all the girls.'

His gaze was steady as he looked at her. 'Yes, I date, but I'm not a notch-carver. I never have been. Forget all this nonsense about Italian men playing the field. This is about you and me.'

This was a conversation she definitely didn't want to have with him. She needed a diversion. Fast. 'Two things, you said. You wanted me to do two things. What was the second?'

'I'm not sure if I should ask you now.'

Her eyes narrowed. 'You might as well spit it out.'

He chuckled. 'That's my Lucy.'

'I'm not *your* Lucy.'

'No. You're your own woman and you're scared of nothing. Except, maybe, yourself,' he said thoughtfully.

She lifted her chin. 'I want to go home.'

'I'll call you a taxi.'

'Thank you.'

He walked over to the phone and paused with his hand on the receiver. 'The second thing, by the way—I wanted to dance with you.'

Her throat dried. 'Dance with me?'

'Mmm-hmm. By moonlight.' The sun had set and the dusk was deepening to the point where he really needed to switch a light on. Except he hadn't: he'd left the curtains open so that moonlight flooded the room. He moistened his lower lip with his tongue. 'And I'm a poor host, sending you home in a taxi before pudding.'

Oh, that mouth. She wished he hadn't done that thing with his mouth. It made her want him to kiss her again. Kiss her and touch her and take her to paradise. 'It doesn't matter.'

'It does, to me.' He looked at her, his eyes intense. 'If I promise to behave myself, Lucy, will you dance with me before I send you home?'

Say no, she told herself.

Her body had other ideas. Because she nodded. He held out his arms and she stepped into them. Maybe it was the wine, she thought—though she hadn't drunk that much. A glass and a half, tops. No, she was dancing with Nic because she *wanted* to dance with him.

At some point, she wasn't sure when, he'd changed the music. Instead of the haunting tenor serenades, Nic was playing blues with a soft, slow, mournful beat. A sensual beat. One that made her sway in time with him.

He was dancing with her. In the moonlight. Holding her close. Rubbing his cheek against her hair. And when the song changed, he held her closer and started singing along: *Need your love so bad.* He had a good voice, soft and deep and husky and perfectly in tune with the CD he was playing. And it was as if he was singing directly to her rather than crooning along to a favourite record, telling her just how much he wanted her and needed her. Just like that fantasy she'd had about him serenading her, except his voice was even better. It was irresistible. She reached up and touched her lips to his. Just once.

He stopped moving—stopped singing—and kissed her back.

Time came to a halt. The world ceased turning. There was nothing but Nic and the moonlight and the slow, soft music in the background and the way he was kissing her.

And then he broke the kiss. 'Lucy.' His voice was husky with suppressed desire. 'I promised you I wouldn't lay a finger on you. I can't keep that promise much longer, unless I put some distance between us.'

He was giving her the choice. Go home to her cottage and brood—or stay here and make love with him.

It was a choice Jack would never have given her.

It was a choice she couldn't make.

'Nic, I…'

He walked away from her, pulled the curtains and switched on the uplighter in the corner of the room. 'I want you, Lucia *mia*. Very badly. And I think you want me, too. But I'm a man of my word. I promised I wouldn't touch you and I'm not going to push you into something you'll regret later.' He came back to her as if she'd tugged some invisible cord between them, and brushed her cheek with the backs of his fingers. 'I'll call you that taxi.'

'No.'

She felt as shocked as he looked. Had she *really* said that?

'No?' he queried. 'Are you telling me you want to stay?'

'I…'

'Tell me, Lucy,' he pleaded. 'Tell me you want to stay with me. Tell me you want me to make you forget…' He paused, and for a horrible moment she thought he was going to say 'Jack', and then he smiled again. 'Tell me you want me to make you forget the world for a while.'

'Nic, I…' Her throat dried. 'I want you to…to…'

He refused to say it for her. Those dark, soulful eyes gave her their own message. *Say it, and I'll do it.*

'Kiss me. Make love to me,' she said.

CHAPTER SEVEN

NIC kissed her again, his mouth more demanding this time, and Lucy realised that he'd picked her up and was carrying her. Carrying her to his bedroom.

Her temperature rose a notch at the thought of Nic and bed.

He drew the curtains and switched on the bedside lamp. And then as he kissed her again, she stopped thinking altogether, just letting herself feel as he stroked away her clothing, discarding her formal black trousers and cream linen shirt. His own clothes ended in a crumpled heap beside hers—regardless of the fact that his suit trousers were expensively cut and his shirt was pure silk and both needed hanging up—and then she was lying on cool, cool cotton, with his heated, hair-roughened skin pressed against her.

His clever fingers stroked her to fever pitch, until she was writhing and begging him to take her. And then, shockingly, he stopped.

'Lucia *mia*.' The words came out as a husky groan. He picked up her hand and kissed her palm, curling her fingers over it. 'I wasn't intending to do this.'

Was he going to stop now? No. Surely he wasn't going to change his mind? She stared at him in shock. 'Don't—don't you want to?'

'Oh, I want to, all right. I've wanted to see your hair spread over my pillow like this since the first moment I met you. I've wanted to touch you and taste you—you have no idea how many times I've almost turned caveman at work, hoisted you over my shoulder and taken you off to my lair.' His eyes were tortured. 'But there's a small matter of responsibility.'

'Responsibility?' she echoed, dazed.

'Are you on the Pill?' he asked softly.

'No.'

'Then, *carissima*, I can't do what I very, very desperately want to do. I can't make you *mia innamorata*, my lover.'

She didn't understand. 'Why?'

'Because,' he told her, his face a mixture of torment and amusement, 'despite this reputation you seem to think I have, I don't sleep around. I don't keep a stock of condoms on the off-chance I'll find a beautiful woman in my bed. Much as I want to make love with you right now, I wasn't planning to seduce you when I brought you here tonight. I'm not prepared. And neither are you.'

Lucy was silent for a long, long moment. And then she began to laugh. She laughed until her stomach hurt and tears were running down her cheeks. Nic joined her. And when they stopped laughing, she rested her cheek against his chest. 'Oh, Nic. After all this.'

'Lucia *mia*,' he said softly. 'Yes, I've dated. A lot. But I don't sleep around, neither do you. So it's safe in that respect. But I don't think you're ready to carry my baby. We can't take that risk.'

'Of course not.' Carry his baby. No. Surely that wasn't *her* heart fluttering at the words? But—she didn't want children. She didn't want marriage and the inevitable divorce and emotional shrapnel. She wanted her career. She had her life all planned out, step by step—had done for years. Lucy Williams, consultant. Senior consultant. Professor.

Why did it all suddenly sound so empty?

And why was her body urging her to pull Nic's head down to hers again, make him lose control until their bodies were joined and they were both so far outside time and space nothing else mattered?

An urge that was so strong she couldn't deny it. She shifted so that her face was close to his.

'Lucy?'

His pupils were dilated, his voice hoarse. And *she* was the one who was making him lose control.

'Nic.'

He muttered something in Italian and her heart did a crazy somersault. Even the sound of his voice turned her on. And she was in his bed. Naked. With him. Skin to skin. She leaned forward and kissed the tip of his nose.

'Lucy, we—'

She stopped his words the quick way. By placing her mouth over his and sliding her tongue between his lips. She could feel his body tensing and smiled inwardly. This was what she wanted. Right here, right now. Niccolo Alberici. Her man.

Before she knew it, she was lying back against his pillows and Nic's clever fingers were caressing her body, coaxing a response from her. She arched against him and he murmured something against her skin—something Italian, so even if she'd caught the words she wouldn't have understood completely. Though as his fingers teased her, playing her body like some cherished instrument in the hands of a master, she found herself whimpering his name. 'Nic. Please.'

'Ah, Lucia *mia*.' And then he was off in Italian again, murmuring husky endearments against her skin. Teasing her nipples until she thought she'd die with longing. And finally kissing his way down over the slight swell of her abdomen.

Surely he wasn't intending to...?

He was. He did. And Lucy cried out as her climax hit

her, a climax stronger than anything she'd felt before in her life.

'Lucia *mia*.' He shifted to lie beside her and cradled her against him.

'Nic.' She held him close. 'What you just did... Thank you.'

'*Prego*. The pleasure was mine too,' he told her softly.

'Not quite. I should...repay the compliment,' she said, her voice shaking.

'You don't owe me anything, Lucia *mia*.' He kissed the tip of her nose. 'Though I wish to hell I lived up to my reputation and had something here so I could make love to you properly.'

'Me, too.'

'Ah, Lucy, if you knew what that just did to me...' He paused. 'There is a way.'

'How?'

'The supermarket across town's open all night. If I, um, take the car and buy...supplies...would you stay until I get back?'

Her eyes widened in surprise. He'd just brought her to the most stunning climax she'd ever had. So unselfishly. Not expecting anything in return—a million miles away from her experiences with Jack. And he thought she was going to disappear? 'Do you honestly think I'd run out on you now?'

'I don't know,' he said. 'Right now, you're here in my bed—exactly how I want you to be, your mouth red with my kisses and your eyes almost black with passion—but if I leave you alone, give you time to think...will you still be here when I get back? Or will you have turned back into my incredibly talented, incredibly sensible registrar and be buttoned back into your suit?'

'Nic.' She rubbed his lower lip with the pad of her

thumb, and he drew her thumb into his mouth and sucked it. 'Oh…I can't think straight when you're around.'

He released her thumb. 'You could come with me.'

'And buy…supplies?'

'No. I wouldn't ask you to do that.' He rubbed his nose against hers. 'There is another way I could keep you here.'

'Such as?'

'Give me thirty seconds.' He pulled on his shirt—now spectacularly crumpled—and a pair of jeans, then raced from the room. She heard crashing and banging. And then he was standing before her with a tub of blueberry Cornish ice cream and a teaspoon and a wide, wide smile.

She inspected the label. 'Not Italian ice cream?'

He grinned. 'I don't have *everything* Italian. Remember, I'm half-English as well.' He bent to kiss her briefly. 'Don't eat it all. I'll be back in ten minutes. Wait for me?'

She nodded. 'Yes. I'll wait for you.'

'Ten minutes, Lucia *mia*. And then…'

He didn't have to say it. She knew exactly what he meant. And her whole body thrilled at the idea.

Nic felt like a teenager as he drove to the supermarket. The feeling only intensified as the young girl at the checkout rang his purchase through and gave him a speculative look. Then he realised how rumpled he probably looked—he'd dragged on a pair of jeans and his shirt at record speed, the shirt wasn't buttoned in the right places, he wasn't wearing any socks and he hadn't bothered with a jacket, despite the coolness of the October night.

Given what he was buying, it was obvious to the whole world why he was in such a rush and what was going to happen in a few minutes' time. What had been happening only a few minutes before.

He could only thank his lucky stars that no one from the

hospital was there to see it. The hospital rumour machine had more than enough material to work on, without him adding to it. Lucy would never, ever live it down.

He gave the checkout girl his sweetest smile and headed for home.

Would Lucy still be there? She'd said she would wait for him. But now she'd had time to reflect on the situation, would she have changed her mind and called a taxi? Would she have left him a note? Something cool and precise, saying she was sorry but this really wasn't a good idea and she was sure they'd manage to work together as colleagues tomorrow?

No way could he be just her colleague on the ward. Not now. Not now he'd seen her eyes as she'd come. Not now she'd cried out his name as she'd climaxed. He wanted everything. The moon, the stars, the universe—and he'd trade the whole lot for that single moment with Lucy and still know he'd got the better bargain.

His pulse accelerated as he parked the car. He just about remembered to flick the button on the keypad to lock it, and rushed back to his flat.

'Lucy?' he called softly as he closed the front door behind him.

She appeared in the kitchen doorway, wearing his navy blue towelling dressing-gown, her hair still loose over her shoulders, and his heart missed a beat.

'Well, hello, there,' she said.

'You stayed.'

She nodded. 'I left you *some* of the ice cream—I put it back in the freezer. I hope you don't mind, but I took a quick shower while you were gone.'

His heart missed another beat as he thought about her in his shower. About joining her there.

She was still here.

'You're quite, quite sure about this, Lucy?' he asked carefully.

She nodded again. 'I'm sure.'

He smiled. 'I feel somewhat overdressed.'

She folded her arms and leaned against the doorjamb. 'So what are you going to do about it, sweetheart?' she drawled in her best Mae West impersonation.

For a long, long moment, they just looked at each other. And then Nic smiled again. 'Wait there.' Nic went over to the stereo, selected a CD then disappeared into his bedroom.

Lucy waited. What was he planning? As he emerged from his bedroom again, she stared in surprise and delight. He was wearing his highwayman's hat. Not the domino mask and the cloak—she felt a twinge of disappointment that he'd left them behind—but the jeans and silk shirt did very, very nicely. The old, faded denim was just as close-fitting as the black trousers he'd worn that night and the white shirt set off his dark complexion to perfection.

Even better, now she knew what he looked like underneath his clothes...

He pressed a switch on the remote control and the music began to play. Lucy almost laughed out loud as she recognised it—'You Can Leave Your Hat On'.

Nic kicked off his shoes and began to dance, his hips weaving sinuously. As he danced, he unbuttoned his shirt and turned his back to her. He turned his head and gave her a broad wink, then slowly eased the white silk over his shoulders.

Lucy really, really couldn't help licking her lips.

He was perfect. Utterly, utterly perfect. His muscles were beautifully toned and his back was beautiful—even more so than the Raphael drawing of Michaelangelo's *David* which her sister Allie had had pinned on their bedroom wall when they'd been teenagers.

He dropped the shirt on the floor, spun round to face her and slowly began to unbutton his jeans, still in time to the music.

Lucy's knees went weak and she was forced to lean back against the wall so she wouldn't fall over. The front view was every bit as good as the back—that beautiful olive skin, the dark sprinkling of hair on his chest, the perfect six-pack. And—her stomach tightened—the arrowing of hair that disappeared beneath the waistband of his jeans...

She grinned as again he turned his back to her and let his jeans fall to the floor.

And then he glanced over his shoulder and blew her a kiss.

'Lucia *mia*,' he said softly. 'Come to me.'

On legs that she thought for a moment would refuse to carry her, she made her way slowly towards him.

He turned to face her. 'Now you're the one who's over-dressed, *mia innamorata*.'

She folded her arms and repeated her earlier challenge. 'So what are you going to do about it?'

'*Permesso?*' he asked in that husky, sexy voice.

'Yes. Oh, yes,' she breathed. She'd wondered once if he made love in Italian or English. Now she knew. And she found the words unbelievably exciting; she didn't under-stand the words themselves, but their meaning was very plain.

'Oh, Lucia. Lucia *mia*. *Bellissima*,' he said as he untied the belt and slowly eased the robe over her shoulders. He bent his head and kissed the rounded curve of her shoul-ders, the dip of her collar-bones. She tipped her head back and he kissed her throat, his lips making tiny fires spring up in each nerve end.

The robe pooled on the floor. And then Nic picked her up, carrying her as easily as if she were a feather.

He was still wearing the hat. The hat that had started everything, when the highwayman had accosted her at the ball.

'My highwayman,' she said, dipping her head beneath the brim of his hat so she could kiss him.

'*Mia principessa*,' he murmured—my princess—and carried her back to his bed.

This time, when his mouth and hands had aroused her to fever pitch, they didn't have to stop. Or compromise. When he paused to protect her, it felt like a lifetime. She wanted him now, now, now. And when he entered her, Lucy felt as if her world was complete, for the very first time in her life.

'Ah, Nic.'

'*Ti piace?* You like that?' he asked softly as he moved.

'Oh, yes.'

'*Mi bacii*,' he said. 'Kiss me, Lucy.'

She shook her head. 'No.'

'No?' He stayed very, very still.

She gave him a lazy grin. 'No. *Mi bacii*, Nic,' she said huskily. 'Now.'

'We'll have to work on that accent, Dr Williams,' he said, nuzzling her mouth. 'I'll have to give you lessons. *Lots* of lessons.'

She gasped as he changed the tempo of his thrusts. 'Yes,' she hissed, arching up to meet him.

'Ah, Lucia *mia*. I've wanted this since the first moment I saw you. My princess…' He lapsed into Italian again.

She had no idea what he was saying, but it was as sexy as hell, hearing him murmuring against her skin. And then she stopped thinking as he kissed her again and changed

the tempo again, taking it slowly until she was begging him
to take her, take her over the edge.

And he did.

'We're going to have to renegotiate this no-touching rule,'
Nic said, some time later, when Lucy was finally capable
of rational thought.

'Oh?'

'Mmm-hmm. After that, I'd say you were definitely my
girl. Wouldn't you?'

She gave him a playful punch. 'That sounded incredibly
smug.'

'I *feel* incredibly smug,' he told her, leaning over to drop
a kiss on her lips. 'What just happened between us… It's
never happened to me before.'

She looked at him in disbelief. 'Are you trying to tell
me you were a virgin?'

He chuckled. 'No. I haven't been a monk—but I haven't
been a playboy either. I've always been very selective. I
suppose what I'm trying to say is…' He lapsed into Italian.

'I'm still on Italian for beginners,' Lucy reminded him.
'Not advanced conversation. Just about all I know is "*mi
bacii*".'

'If you insist.' He kissed her lingeringly.

She was shivering when he lifted his head again. 'Not
fair. I can't think straight when you do that.'

He rubbed his thumb along her lower lip. 'You're the
one who told me to kiss you. In Italian, no less. So now I
know what to do when we have a fight.'

'When, not if?'

He shrugged. 'You're stubborn and opinionated. And
don't try to protest, you know you are. And I'm half-Italian.
We're bound to fight, at some point.' His eyes held a
wicked gleam. 'But at least we'll enjoy making up.' He

coiled a strand of her hair in his fingers. 'Why do you always pin this back at work?'

'Hygiene.'

'I bet you wear it pinned back out of work, too.'

She flushed. 'Habit.'

'Hmm. Perhaps, *mia innamorata*, I should teach you some new habits.' He lapsed into Italian again.

'I think you're lucky I didn't understand a word of that,' Lucy told him.

He stroked her cheek. 'My apologies, *mia principessa*. When I get emotional, the Italian side of me takes over.'

'Mmm, I had noticed,' she teased.

'For that, *you* make the coffee.'

She shook her head. 'Uh-uh. I'm the guest.'

'And I'm forgetting my manners.' His eyes crinkled at the corners. 'But I don't think I could bear to leave you in bed for long enough to make coffee. Not even instant coffee.'

'You have *instant* coffee in your flat?' Considering his scathing comments about the coffee at Treverro General—with the exception of the mochaccinos at Pat's Place—she couldn't quite believe that.

'No,' he admitted. 'The quickest thing I can offer is coffee ice cream.'

Lucy chuckled. 'You know all my weaknesses.'

'And you mine.' He lapsed into Italian again.

'Translate,' she demanded.

'Ice cream.'

'Even *I* know that's "*gelati*",' Lucy said.

He pressed a kiss into her palm and curled her fingers over it. 'Give me thirty seconds.'

He fetched the ice cream and a teaspoon, and fed her spoonful by spoonful, making her reach up for it and then 'accidentally' dripping ice cream on her so he had to lick it from her skin. She grabbed the spoon and retaliated, and the ice cream was quickly forgotten as teasing became caresses and caresses turned into love-making.

And afterwards, she let him lead her to the shower. Soap her all over. Wash her glorious hair—and make love with her again.

'I can't get enough of you, Lucy,' he said. And switched to Italian. '*Lucia del mio cuore*. Lucy of my heart. I want time to stop. I want this moment to last for ever, this perfection of being with you.'

This time, she didn't ask him to translate. She kissed him.

They ended up back in Nic's bed. 'Will you stay with me tonight, Lucy?' he asked.

She moved restlessly against him. 'I should go. My clothes are at home—I don't even have a toothbrush with me.'

He kissed her hair. 'I'll get up early tomorrow and buy you one from the supermarket.'

'I can't go to work in the clothes I was wearing today.'

'You don't have to. You're on a late tomorrow. I'm on early so I'll drive you home after breakfast,' he promised. 'Stay with me? Please?'

She was still for a long, long moment, and then relaxed against him. 'All right. I'll stay.'

'*Grazie*,' he said softly. '*Mia innamorata*.'

CHAPTER EIGHT

THE phone shrilled insistently. Lucy reached out automatically—and opened her eyes in shock when the phone wasn't where it should have been, on her bedside cabinet.

Because this wasn't her bed.

It was Nic Alberici's.

And her legs were still entwined with his, though his body was no longer cradled round hers. He was sitting upright. He'd grabbed the phone from his side of the bed and had thrust one hand through his rumpled hair. 'Maternal tachycardia—any shock? What about the contractions? Any sign of foetal distress? Right. Previous labour? Oh, hell. Yes, I'm coming in. Right now.'

Gently, he disentangled his body from Lucy's and got out of bed, still talking on the cordless phone. 'Give her oxygen at fifteen litres a minute—I want a tight-fitting mask with a reservoir—and cross-match six units of blood. If you see any signs of shock, get a transfusion in fast. Has she got an epidural in? Good. Get it topped up to the max. Get in touch with Theatre, tell them I'm going to do an emergency section and I'll need to do a laparotomy as well, so I can see how bad it is and whether I can repair it or if I'll have to do a hysterectomy. OK. Yes, I'll talk to her husband. I'll be there in ten minutes.'

'Uterine rupture?' Lucy guessed as Nic started to pull his clothes on. It was rare in the UK—around one in fifteen hundred deliveries—but she recognised the symptoms Nic had described.

'Yes. Caesarean scar dehiscence. Apparently the mum

had been upset by all this too-posh-to-push nonsense she'd read in the papers and decided she was going to have a vaginal delivery this time at any cost. She moved here before her second pregnancy and didn't tell us her full history in case we made her have another section. Somehow it was missed when she went into labour. And she only told the midwife when it was too late.' He raked a hand through his hair. 'I'm sorry, Lucy. I have to go in. I know I said I'd take you back to your place this morning. And I wanted to bring you breakfast in bed. I was going to get hot croissants from the local bakery, but—'

'Go,' she interrupted him gently. 'I can ring for a taxi home. It won't kill me if I don't clean my teeth until I get back to my place.'

'I'll see you when you get in. Have lunch with me?'

'If you're out of Theatre by then.'

Nic kissed her lightly. 'I don't want to leave you.'

'I know. But you're needed on the ward, and I know that, too. I ought to be there with you really.'

He shook his head. 'You're not on call. I am. Help yourself to breakfast, bath, shower—whatever you want. The fridge is full and there's plenty of hot water. The door's on a latch so you don't need to worry about a key—just close the door behind you. And I'll see you at lunchtime, *mia principessa*.' He kissed her again. '*Ciao*.'

'*Ciao*,' she echoed.

It felt strange, being in Nic's flat without him there. She definitely couldn't spend the morning lying in his bed, tempting though it was to roll over and get some sleep. They hadn't slept much last night—they'd dozed for a while and ended up making love again.

Lucy smiled at the memory. Nic was a generous lover. He'd been concerned for her pleasure, and he'd held her so close afterwards, cherishing her. If she closed her eyes now, she could almost imagine he was still beside her, the bed still warmed by his body heat and his clean male scent on the sheets.

But she really ought call a taxi and go home to change before her shift. Not to mention checking whether her bike was still safely at the hospital. And facing the Hammonds again.

Her heart skipped a beat. Jack. Would he leave her alone, now he thought she was with Nic?

And what about Nic himself? Last night had been incredible, but had it been the same for him? Or was she just a temporary diversion, another in his long line of three-dates-and-you're-out women? By the time she went on duty, would he have changed?

'You're just being paranoid, Lucy,' she told herself. 'Not all men are like Jack. Stop analysing and live for the moment, for once in your life. Everything's going to be fine.'

'So you finally melted the ice maiden, then.' Mal gave his boss a broad wink.

'Excuse me?'

Mal missed the warning note in Nic's voice. 'Just what she needed. Not that she'd ever have given any of us the chance to do it.' He grinned. 'So what was she—?'

'If you say anything remotely like that to her,' Nic cut in, 'and I find out about it—which, believe me, I will— you'll be out of this rotation straight away without a reference. Understand?'

'Hey, no need to be so touchy!'

'I just think your senior registrar deserves a little bit more respect. Don't you?' Nic asked.

Mal flushed dully and mumbled a response.

'Good. Now, I have an emergency in Theatre. I trust

you're not going to delay me any further.' Nic gave him a wintry look and strode off to Theatre.

Though Mal's words had brought home the reality of the situation. Nic had made love with Lucy. His closest colleague—his number two on the ward. Professionally, it was the most stupid thing he could have done, compromising their relationship at work. He'd never even dated a colleague from the same ward, let alone slept with one. Everyone knew it made life too complicated. So why, why, *why* had he done it? And with the most senior of his staff, too?

Personally, it was even more of a mess. Because of Lucy's ex. Supposing Jack hadn't been there on the ward, hadn't kissed her or tried to push her into something she'd said she didn't want…would Lucy still have slept with Nic last night? Or had she just got carried away in the heat of the moment and taken their smokescreen a bit too far?

Then a worse thought hit him. Had he just been a substitute for Jack, the man Lucy really wanted but couldn't have because he was married to someone else? When he himself had made love with her, she'd called out his name—but had she really been seeing Jack's face? And when she'd had time to think about what had happened between them, would she regret it?

Adrenalin tingled in his fingers. Facing her wasn't going to be easy, when he didn't know how she was going to react. Or how *he* was going to react, for that matter. They'd rushed into it, gone for what they'd both wanted right there and right then—but neither of them had thought of the consequences.

They hardly knew each other. Yes, Lucy was the most gorgeous woman he'd ever met and when they'd made love it had been better than he'd ever known—but it was still too soon to know if she was The One. Or for her to know if he was The One for her. They hadn't even been on a proper date—he'd simply cooked her a meal, danced with her and rushed her into his bed.

How stupid could he get?

He didn't even know where they could start trying to sort this out.

But he was needed in Theatre. He had to concentrate on his patient. For now, the situation between him and Lucy would have to wait. Maybe they should give each other some space to work out what they really wanted. He'd talk to her about it later.

Taking a deep breath, he went into the scrub room and started to get ready.

Nina was the first on Lucy's rounds. To Lucy's relief, Jack wasn't there. 'He's gone to have a cup of coffee and read the paper. I think he's a bit bored, hanging round the hospital,' Nina confided. 'And it's the second day of our holiday. He'd got so many things planned. It's such a shame that he's going to miss out on them. Can't you let me go a bit earlier?'

'How are you feeling?' Lucy asked.

'Fine. Really good.'

Lucy looked at the chart and didn't like what she saw. 'Your temperature's up a bit.'

'Only because it's hot in here.'

'Hmm.' Lucy took the thermometer from the holder by Nina's bed. 'Let me check this again.' She looked at the reading and shook her head. 'I'm sorry, Nina. Your temperature's up and I really don't want to discharge you just yet, just in case you've picked up an infection. It's quite common after a cerclage and you've come this far—why take risks now?'

'I suppose.' Nina's voice was thick with disappointment.

'Jack's not going to be happy about having to hang around here even longer.'

I'm not happy about him hanging around either, Lucy thought. But she was a doctor. She couldn't discharge a patient who might be at risk, just because the situation unsettled her. Nina clearly didn't know anything about Jack's past with Lucy and it wasn't her fault that her husband was a complete louse.

Lucy examined Nina carefully. 'I can't see any other obvious signs, but I'd rather not take the risk. I'm sorry, Nina. If you'd like a second opinion…'

Nina smiled. 'From that gorgeous Mr Alberici, by any chance?'

Lucy flushed, and Nina's smile broadened. 'I thought there was something going on. Jack said as much last night.'

'What?' Lucy blurted. Surely Jack hadn't told Nina about them? No, he couldn't have done. If Nina knew everything, she wouldn't be talking to Lucy so easily.

'He said you two were, well…snatching a bit of time together. It must be difficult, working together.'

'It is,' Lucy admitted. And it would be even harder now she'd actually slept with him.

'You're *so* lucky. He's even more handsome than my Jack,' Nina added in a whisper. 'And that voice! He could talk Italian to me any time.'

Lucy shifted uncomfortably. 'Well, I'll be back to see you later. But I think Nic will say the same as I do about your temperature.'

'I suppose it's better to lose another day of the holiday than to risk the baby,' Nina said. 'Maybe Jack can do a bit of sightseeing on his own.'

'I'm sure he'd rather be with you,' Lucy said.

Nina shook her head. 'He doesn't like hospitals. I think

he's scared of them, though he won't admit it,' she confided. 'My mum's going to be my birth partner. I think
he'd pass out!'

'Men,' Lucy said, and took her leave before Jack could
come back and demand a private discussion with her. Right
now, Jack Hammond was the last person she wanted to see.
Except possibly for Nic. Because if she'd made her usual
mess of things, shown her usual hideous lack of judgement
where men were concerned, Nic wouldn't want to have
anything to do with her now she'd slept with him. And that
was way too scary to contemplate.

Lucy was writing up her notes from the rounds at the
nurses' station when Nic came out of Theatre and slumped
on a chair beside her.

'I think today's *my* turn for the day from hell. I need
cake,' he said.

'So how did it go in Theatre?' Rosemary asked, handing
Nic the tin of chocolate biscuits she kept at the nurses'
station.

'The baby's OK—we managed to deliver her before any
real damage was done. But the mum… You know how
more than two-thirds of scar ruptures are repairable. Hers
wasn't. She had a tear right down to her cervix, so I had
to give her a hysterectomy. And she's only twenty-six.
She's not going to be able to have any more children—and
her husband said they were planning four.' He swallowed
hard and crumbled a biscuit between his fingers. 'I had to
get her permission to do it while she was on the operating
table. Her husband was holding her hand at the time—and
he broke down.' He continued fidgeting with the crumbs.
'I'd like her in a side room, Rosemary, if you can manage
it. She needs some space. There isn't any renal damage,
thank God, so I've written up intravenous antibiotics.'

'How's she coping?' Lucy asked.

'Not well. She's going to need counselling. So's her husband. And it wouldn't surprise me if one or both of them ended up with depression after this.' Nic raked a hand through his hair. 'It's such a bloody *mess*. The sad thing is, it needn't have happened. If only she'd told us about it right at the start.'

'Do you want me to have a word with her health visitor and community midwife?' Lucy asked.

He shook his head. 'I'll do it. If only she'd talked to us about her fears, told us the truth about her last pregnancy. We could have reassured her that it's possible to have a vaginal birth after a section, depending on why she needed a section last time. If it had been for something that wouldn't necessarily happen in this pregnancy, too, we could have given her a trial of labour and kept more of a watchful eye on her.' He shook his head, clearly distressed and angry. 'Why the hell didn't anyone notice her scar before?'

'It's not your fault, Nic,' Rosemary said.

'It feels like it is. I'm the consultant. I should have made sure.' He sighed. 'I need someone to moan to. Come and have a late lunch with me, Lucy?'

'Go on,' Rosemary said, before Lucy could protest. 'We'll bleep you if we need you.'

'What a woman. Rosemary, *carissima*, if you weren't already married…' Nic teased.

Lucy's stomach tightened. After what had happened between them last night, he was flirting with Rosemary?

Lighten up, she told herself silently. It's the way he is. He doesn't mean anything by it. And he hasn't ignored you, has he?

Though he hadn't actually said much to her. Nothing that wasn't work-related.

On the other hand, he wouldn't have asked her to have lunch with him if he was going to avoid her…would he?

'You OK?' Nic asked as they headed for Pat's Place.

'Yes.'

'But?'

Lucy wasn't going to admit to her fears about him. She took refuge in work. 'I was hoping to discharge Nina Hammond today, but her temperature's up.'

'Infection?'

'Might be. There aren't any other signs right now, but I'd rather keep an eye on her, so if it is we can catch it early,' Lucy said.

'Though it means Jack's going to be around for a while longer.'

She nodded.

He shrugged. 'So be it.'

She couldn't read the look on his face, but she wasn't sure she wanted to know what he was thinking right now. Supposing he'd changed his mind about her? She couldn't ask him to keep the smokescreen going until Jack had left. She'd have the worst of both worlds—Jack refusing to leave her alone, and the most embarrassing kind of awkwardness between her and Nic at work.

Her stomach dived. All in all, yesterday might just have topped the league table headed 'Lucy's worst mistakes'…

No. She was being paranoid. Nic had had a rough morning in Theatre. That was why they were here now—he needed her to do the same thing he'd done for her yesterday. Provide coffee, cake and sympathy.

'Go and find us a table,' she said, 'and I'll get you some cake.'

She was choosing a selection of muffins when she heard a voice behind her in the queue. 'Off with loverboy again, are we?'

She stiffened. 'That's none of your business, Jack.'

'Oh, it is. Because we've got unfinished business, Lucy,' he whispered, his breath fanning her ear.

She gave a mirthless laugh and pulled back from him. 'I don't think so. Jack, your wife is in my ward, after nearly miscarrying your child. Doesn't that mean anything to you?'

His face twisted. 'Yes, of course it does—but Nina doesn't really want me. She just wants a baby. It's all she's thought about for years. That's what I've been trying to tell you. Nina'll be OK, just her and the baby. It's what she wants. Our marriage was virtually over anyway.'

Jack honestly expected her to believe that—when she'd seen with her own eyes how Nina looked adoringly at him, had heard his wife chattering about their plans for the future?

She went cold. How many times had he used that line before? How many times had he been unfaithful to *her*?

'Lucy, I know I've hurt you, but I'm going to make it up to you. We're going to be together and I'm going to make you happy.'

Lucy wasn't sure whether to laugh or throw something at him. 'Jack, stop being stupid and go back to your wife. She needs you.'

'But *I* need *you*,' Jack said.

Lucy shook her head. 'All you need,' she told him, 'is to grow up. Learn to deal with your responsibilities instead of running away and letting someone else pick up the pieces. I'm not interested in you, Jack. Not now, not ever. There is no you and me—and there isn't going to be either.'

'But, Lucy—'

'Tell me,' Lucy said, driven beyond her patience with him, 'what's so hard to understand about the word "no"?'

'You don't mean it.'

'Oh, but I do. I don't love you, Jack. I don't want you. I don't need you. You have no place in my life. And I'm looking you straight in the eye as I'm saying it. So believe it.'

'That smarmy Italian isn't right for you,' Jack burst out.

'It's *half*-Italian, actually,' Nic said, appearing beside them. 'And that's for Lucy to decide, not you.' He placed a hand on Lucy's shoulder. 'Everything OK, Lucia *mia*?'

'Yes. I think Mr Hammond here was asking for a second opinion.'

'I trust my registrar's judgement. From what Lucy's told me, she's right not to take any risks with your wife's condition.' Nic's smile didn't reach his eyes. 'And I've already asked you to leave my staff alone, Mr Hammond. Perhaps I didn't make myself clear.'

'My staff', Lucy noted. Not 'my girl'. Though Jack didn't seem to notice the difference. He simply shot Nic a poisonous look and left the café.

'I'll take a rain-check on the cake, Lucy. I'm really not in the mood,' Nic said, taking his hand from Lucy's shoulder. 'But don't feel you have to rush back to the ward. You're entitled to your break.'

And then he was gone. Just like that.

Lucy stared after him in disbelief. What was going on? Nic had virtually dragooned her into having lunch with him—why had he suddenly stomped off before he'd had anything to eat or drink?

Please, no, she begged silently. Please, don't let me have made the same mistake again. Please, don't let me have found myself another Jack, someone who's only interested in the thrill of the chase and gets bored in two seconds flat.

Three dates and you're out.

But she and Nic hadn't even had one proper date, really. Just sex.

What the hell had she done?

CHAPTER NINE

THE day got worse, because Nic seemed to be actively avoiding her.

You're overreacting. He's just playing it cool at work to stop us being the focus of gossip, Lucy told herself. He's being sensible about things.

But when he'd left at the end of his shift without saying a word to her or leaving her a message, a nasty, cold feeling squirmed its way down her spine. And when she left at the end of her own shift to find no message from him in her locker or on her answering-machine at home, the cold feeling spread to her stomach as she realised what was really going on.

Nic had slept with her and dumped her. He hadn't even had the courtesy to tell her to her face.

She had indeed found herself another Jack.

As nights went, Lucy rated it as one of the worst she'd spent—worse even than that terrible night four years ago. Every time she closed her eyes, she saw Nic. Remembered the passion in his eyes, the way he'd made love with her. The way he'd lied to her.

The worst thing was, she'd believed him. She'd allowed herself to think that there really was such a thing as happiness. That she and Nic maybe had a future. And now she knew the truth: the whole thing was a sham. She'd made a fool of herself in public again, because the whole ward was gossiping about the affair between them. Tomorrow, they'd be speculating about why it had blown over so quickly—why Lucy hadn't even lasted more than one date.

She was never, ever, ever going to put herself in that position again. From now on, her job would be her life. It would be enough.

It had to be.

She'd gone past the stage of tears, but she slept badly. The next morning, her eyes were sore and gritty from lack of sleep, her head hurt, no amount of teeth-cleaning could take the nasty taste from her mouth and the idea of going into work and facing everyone made her stomach heave. But her reputation as an ice maiden would stop the gossip soon enough. All she had to do was smile politely and be professional and pretend she didn't give a damn.

All.

But she'd forgotten about Mal, whose first comment to her was, 'Wow. Heavy night with His Lordship, was it?'

'I beg your pardon?' Lucy's eyes widened with anger.

'He doesn't look any better than you do! Maybe you two ought to have…' he gave her a salacious grin '…a night off.'

Anger ripped through Lucy. Normally, she'd have ignored him or made some cutting comment, but this…this, on top of the miserable night she'd spent wishing herself a million miles away, was too much! 'Sister's office. Now.'

'Luce—'

'Now,' she said, her voice low and measured, her control belying the depth of her fury.

'Luce, I was only—' he began as she closed the door to Rosemary's office behind them.

'Having a laugh?' she cut in. 'Malcolm, I've cut you a lot of slack in the past. I've put up with your jokes and your teasing and all the rest of it. But it's time you grew up. You're my SHO. By now, you're supposed to be past the student prank stage.'

'Hey, I didn't mean—'

'No, you never do. But you need to learn there's a time and a place for jokes. If you do it all the time, it's wearing. More than wearing. And working with you is starting to become like a long, tiring labour with no pain relief. It's not funny, it's not clever and I've had enough. You've got the potential to be a great doctor. Don't screw it up because you think you're a comedian.'

'Lucy, I...' He shifted uncomfortably. 'I don't know what to say.'

'Try nothing, for a change,' she told him. 'Try thinking of other people before you open your mouth.'

'I'm sorry.'

She put her hands on her hips and glared at him. 'And you can stop spreading rumours about me and Nic Alberici. I work with him, just as I work with you. End of story.'

'OK, boss.'

Her eyes narrowed. 'And less of the flippancy.'

This time, he didn't make a comment—simply flushed, nodded, and followed her meekly back out of Rosemary's office.

At least she didn't have to put up with Jack today. That was one small mercy. 'He's gone for a drive,' Nina said. 'I think he said something about finding a golf course, whacking a few balls across the fairway. He's fed up, being stuck here all the time.'

'And you're feeling just as stir-crazy, stuck in that bed,' Lucy said.

'Yes. But I know you're not going to let me move until my temperature comes down.' Nina smiled wryly. 'I thought about sticking ice in my mouth and across my fore-head.'

Lucy chuckled, despite her inner misery. 'Sneaky! But your temperature's down on what it was. Give it until to-morrow. Just to be on the safe side.'

'If it goes on much longer, I'll have to take up knitting,' Nina grumbled good-naturedly.

Nic reviewed the set of notes on his desk and frowned. This wasn't like Lucy. He was used to her neat, precise writing and short but detailed notes. He flicked through another set. And another. Her last lot of reports were slap-dash, to say the least. Even Mal's notes made more sense. He was going to have to have a word with her about it.

Yet another reason why he should never have got in-volved with Lucy. Having a chat about work standards with junior staff had never been his favourite task—he enjoyed teaching and the moments when his younger colleagues suddenly grasped the point and were illuminated, but hav-ing to tear strips off people for sloppy work was something he really, really hated doing. The fact that the member of staff in question had slept with him and could take his comments personally instead of professionally made it even worse.

Hell. He was trying to give Lucy space to work out what she wanted; he needed space to work out what *he* wanted, too. One more day, he decided. He'd give her one more day—and if her reports tomorrow were like these, instead of her usual high standard, he'd tackle the problem. In the meantime, he'd do an unobtrusive second round after her to make sure the patients were getting the care they needed.

Lucy and Nic exchanged polite nods when they came across each other, but neither said a thing that didn't involve a patient. Not even the pleasantries that most of the staff exchanged.

So this is how it's going to be, she thought miserably. Cold and just the right side of civil. But what other option did she have? To leave the hospital, find herself a job somewhere else? And she'd been happy here, until Nic. She loved her job and she loved Cornwall and she loved her cottage. She didn't want to give it all up and start again somewhere else.

She managed to avoid Nic for most of her shift—until what had started as a straightforward delivery suddenly became difficult, and Gemma called for her help.

'Lucy, I know you're just off home, but Nic's not answering his bleeper and—'

'That's what I'm here for,' Lucy said gently. She was aware that everyone in the unit had been treading very carefully around her all day—no doubt, Mal had regaled everyone with the story of how she'd suddenly become the scariest doctor in the hospital. Though Lucy liked to think they'd all worked with her for long enough to know she was perfectly approachable and she'd never, ever let a patient down. 'What's up?'

'I think I've got a mum here with a retained placenta— her name's Tracy Johnson. We agreed to do a managed third stage and I gave her oxytocin, but she's been in third stage for twenty minutes now.'

Lucy knew that in the third stage of labour—the delivery of the placenta—most placentas were delivered within ten minutes. If it hadn't been delivered within thirty minutes of a managed labour, it was likely to need manual removal. The main danger with a retained placenta was the potential risk of a large bleed, followed by an infection.

'I'm a bit worried about doing cord traction,' Gemma said.

Lucy nodded. 'Yes—we don't want the cord to snap or her uterus to invert. What kind of pain relief did she have?' She crossed her fingers. Please, please, don't let it have been a gas-and-air or pethidine delivery. Please, let it have been an epidural.

'Epidural.'

Lucy realised then that she'd been holding her breath. 'Well, that's one good thing—we won't need a general anaesthetic.' All they had to do was top up the epidural anaesthesia. 'But you'll need to bleep the anaesthetist, cross-match a couple of units of blood and get me a consent form, please.'

'Will do.'

Lucy went into the delivery room and introduced herself to Tracy. 'From what Gemma tells me, your placenta might not have separated properly, so I might need to give you a bit of extra help to finish off the last stage. Would you mind if I examined you?'

Tracy nodded. 'I'm just so tired—I just want it all over with and a cuddle with my baby.'

'You've done really well,' Lucy said, palpating Tracy's abdomen. It was still bulky, so Lucy knew the placenta hadn't separated. 'What I'm going to do now is try to get your body to do the last little bit of work. I'm going to rub up a contraction, and we'll get your baby to help out a bit, too—if he suckles, it'll stimulate your body to produce a hormone that'll help deliver your placenta.'

After three more minutes, by which time Lucy had helped Tracy latch her son onto her breast and Gemma had returned with Ray Edwards, the anaesthetist, there was no sign of the placenta moving. Lucy sighed inwardly. 'Tracy, it's not going to shift. I need to remove it manually. Can I have your consent, please?'

Gemma handed Lucy the form, and Tracy duly signed

it. Ray topped up the epidural, Gemma swaddled the baby and put him back in his crib and Lucy put Tracy in the lithotomy position. She placed one hand on the abdomen to stabilise the uterus, then gently inserted her other hand into the cervix, following the cord to find the placenta. If she couldn't work it free from the uterus—a condition known as placenta accreta, which was rare but every obstetrician's nightmare—Tracy would need a hysterectomy. 'Can you ask someone to bleep Nic and get him on standby?' she asked Gemma.

Gemma nodded and hurried off.

Lucy located the placenta and gently began to work it free, using the edge of her hand. 'You're doing really well here, Tracy,' she reassured her patient, though inwardly she was shaking. Please, please, let the placenta separate, she begged silently. If it didn't, it would mean another hysterectomy on another very young mother, and Nic had been upset enough about the last one he'd had to do.

Not that Nic's feelings made any difference to the situation. She didn't care about him any more, she reminded herself.

At last, the placenta separated, and Lucy was able to remove it by cord traction. She examined it carefully. 'It's all complete. Good news.' She smiled at Tracy. 'I'm going to give you some oxytocin now to help your uterus contract down properly, and some antibiotics to make sure you don't pick up an infection.' She wrote up the prescription on Tracy's notes. 'I'd like to keep you in overnight—and I'll be in to see you tomorrow morning, see how you're feeling and how this gorgeous little one's doing.' She stroked the baby's cheek. 'He's beautiful. You did really well.'

'Everything all right?' a voice asked as she left the room.

She looked up at Nic and stiffened her spine. 'Fortunately, yes. We won't need your surgical skills tonight.'

'Good.' He nodded abruptly. 'Ask the midwives for twenty-minute obs and tell them to bleep me if there's any sign of a bleed or her blood pressure dips.'

'Of course.' Lucy just managed to stop herself adding a sarcastic 'sir'. Did he think she wouldn't have already thought of that? She was a senior registrar, not a wet-behind-the-ears student doctor who needed someone to check on her work to make sure the patient was properly cared for.

For a moment, she thought he was going to say something else—and then he turned on his heel and left.

Even though she knew now what a louse he was, it was hard to watch him walk away. 'No might-have-beens, Lucy,' she reminded herself, and went to hang up her white coat before handing over to the next shift.

Even cycling home at top speed didn't improve her mood; she didn't get the usual rush she felt at zooming down the hill towards her cottage. And the red light wasn't blinking on her answering-machine—Nic clearly didn't want to get in touch with her.

She wasn't sure that she wanted to talk to him either. On impulse, she unplugged her phone. If he did ring her, she wouldn't hear it. And if there was an emergency at the hospital, they'd bleep her.

But the evening dragged. She couldn't concentrate on anything, even cooking. For the first time in years, she burned her omelette and had to scrape it into the bin. Not that she felt like eating. Comfort food was out—ice cream reminded her too much of Nic and making love at his flat. She associated chocolate, cake and sweet things with him, too. And she quickly discovered that pummelling a cushion didn't help in the slightest.

*   *   *

By the time she got to work the next day, Lucy felt like an overwound spring. Every muscle was tight with tension and she couldn't concentrate enough to use the relaxation techniques the midwives taught the doctors as well as the mums-to-be.

'Are you all right, Lucy?' Rosemary asked.

'I'm perfectly fine,' Lucy snapped. 'Why does everyone keep asking me that?'

'You just...' Rosemary stopped. 'Never mind. Give me a shout if you want anything.'

'Right.'

Lucy was aware that she was more brusque than normal with her patients on her morning round. And when she came to Nina Hammond and saw Jack's sly grin when she went to Nina's bedside, she only just suppressed her urge to pummel him in the same way she'd pummelled the cushion the previous evening.

Nina, after several days of bed-rest, was itching to be discharged.

'Will you let me out today?' Nina asked. 'Please?'

Lucy checked the observation charts and did a last run-through herself. 'Yes. Though I'd recommend taking it very, very easy for the next few days,' she said. 'How much longer were you planning to stay in Cornwall?'

'Three or four days—weren't we, Jack? We were going to go round the Eden Project. Jack's really into gardens,' Nina said.

He certainly hadn't been when Lucy had known him. People changed, she supposed. Though Jack had already proved he hadn't changed for the better. 'It's a big site and you'd be walking for hours. I really think you'd be better off leaving the Eden Project for your next trip to Cornwall,' Lucy said. 'Do you have a long way to go back home?'

'Five hours or so—depends on the traffic. We live in London,' Nina explained.

'Well, as long as you're not the one doing the driving,' Lucy said. 'Make sure you take plenty of breaks on the journey back.'

'We will.' Nina smiled at her. 'Thank you, Dr Williams. You've been so kind.'

'Just doing my job,' Lucy said.

'You've been fantastic,' Jack said, taking her hand.

She couldn't shake him off in front of Nina. Not without an explanation she didn't much want to give. She gave him her most wintry look and only just resisted the urge to kick him when he rubbed his thumb against her palm. Clearly he thought he was giving her some secret signal.

If only she had long, sharp nails so she could give him one back. A signal that would tell him very clearly to leave her alone.

'I'm sure you'll be only too pleased to get out of here, Nina,' she said. 'Good luck, anyway, and I hope the rest of your pregnancy's plain sailing.'

'Cheers. If it's a girl, we'll call her after you,' Nina said.

Lucy Hammond? Oh, no. Surely Jack wouldn't twist the knife that much? Lucy fervently hoped that the Hammonds had a boy. She gave them what she hoped was a professional smile and left the room.

She decided to take her break before Nic was due in. Maybe a walk in the hospital gardens would clear her mind and she'd be able to face him calmly and professionally. She paced up and down the path by the flower-beds, scowling at the pansies, but she could actually feel her blood pressure rising as she walked. Up and up and up until she was ready to explode.

'Hi, Lucy. I thought I saw you come this way.'

She spun round to face Jack. 'Oh, for heaven's sake! Not you again. Can't you leave me alone?'

'Not now I've seen you again. Not now I've realised what a fool I was. I haven't been able to stop thinking about you. I've tried to stay away, really I have. But we were meant to be together, Lucy. Can't you see it?'

'No, Jack, I can't.'

He grabbed her hands and held them tightly. 'I know I upset you—'

'Upset me?' she cut in. 'You have no idea, do you? I loved you, Jack. I was planning to spend the rest of my life with you.'

'I'm sorry.'

'Sorry isn't enough, Jack. You weren't there when it counted. Do you know what it feels like to stand there at the church in your wedding dress, waiting and hearing all the whispers going on behind you as the guests wonder what the hell is going on? To wonder if maybe there's been some terrible accident and your fiancé's lying in hospital somewhere, seriously hurt or even dead? And then for the vicar to say that he's really sorry, but he can't wait any longer for the groom as there's another couple due to be married and their wedding guests need to be seated if their wedding's to take place on time?'

Anger surged through her. She pulled her hands free and yelled at him, not caring any more if anyone overheard. 'You left me at the altar, Jack. You just didn't turn up. You didn't even leave me so much as a note to tell me why— I had to find out the hard way. You left me to sort out the whole bloody mess because you'd run off to Spain, like the spineless bastard you are! I had to face everyone and return all the wedding presents. I had to explain to everyone. I had to leave the job I loved because of you—it was un- bearable, going into work and seeing all the pitying glances, hearing people stop their conversations every time I walked into the room.' She shook her head in disbelief. 'You ruined my life, Jack.'

Nic, who'd heard the last part of Lucy's speech as he made his way towards them, stopped dead.

So Jack wasn't just Lucy's ex, a persistent and trouble-some former boyfriend who wouldn't take no for an answer.

Jack had jilted her at the altar.

Jack was the man who'd wrecked her life and turned her into an ice maiden.

CHAPTER TEN

'I THINK you'd better go, Hammond,' Nic said coolly, coming to stand protectively next to Lucy. 'Your wife must be waiting in the car for you.'

'That's Lucy's decision, not yours.' Jack lifted his chin. 'Want to make something of it?'

'No. You're not worth it.' Nic put his arm round Lucy. She was shaking uncontrollably and he pulled her back into the strength of his body. 'Come on, Lucy. Let's go.'

For a moment she resisted him, but then she let him lead her away from Jack. The moment they were round the corner, she pulled away. 'I don't want you touching me either.'

Nic sighed. 'We need to talk.'

Said the man who'd barely spoken to her since he'd slept with her. 'I don't think so.'

'About work, among other things. I saw you come out here and I wanted to have a word with you about what's been happening on the ward. And then I saw Jack bothering you.'

'And you decided to come to my rescue. How very, very noble of you.' Her voice dripped scorn. 'What a perfect knight you are.'

Nic raked a hand through his hair. 'Lucy…'

'How much did you hear?' she demanded.

'Enough.'

'Don't you *dare* pity me,' she warned.

'I'm not pitying you. But I wish I'd known.'

'And that would have made a difference?'

'Yes. No. Oh, hell. This is difficult.'

'It's not a bed of roses for me either,' she snarled back.

'I don't want to discuss this in the middle of the hospital grounds. Let's go to the park—somewhere a bit quieter, where we won't be disturbed.'

She looked at him as if he'd just crawled out from under a stone. 'You seriously think I want to go anywhere with you?'

'We need to talk. The park, or my office—your choice. But I'd rather say what I've got to say away from the ward. The last thing either of us need is for someone to overhear this and start the rumour mill churning.'

So this was it. His 'dear Jane' speech. For a nasty moment, Lucy thought that she was going to be sick there and then—bile rose in her throat and she actually felt her stomach heave. She put a hand across her mouth and choked it back.

'Are you all right?'

Of course she wasn't! But she was used to pretending, used to maintaining her cool, calm façade. Years of practice made it easier. She swallowed hard. 'I'm fine,' she lied. 'Let's go to the park.'

They walked in silence across the road to the municipal park. Leaves crunched under their feet. In any other situation, Nic would have taken her hand, teased her into kicking up the leaves with him and reliving her childhood. Having a bit of fun. But what he'd overheard and what he had to say weighed too heavily on him.

He felt like the worst kind of louse, kicking her when she was already down. Pulling the straws from her reach while the current swept her on. But what choice did he have? He was responsible for the ward and right now she was putting the patients at risk. They had to come first.

The park was almost deserted. Nic strode over to a bench and gestured to her to sit down.

Lucy folded her arms. 'Spit it out, then.'

He bit his lip. 'I feel a complete bastard, saying this to you when you're already so upset—but I think you ought to take a few days' leave.'

'What?' Lucy stared at him, clearly not believing what she'd just heard. 'Are you suspending me?'

'Not formally. Just giving you some space.'

'But—I don't understand.'

'You're an A-1 doctor, Lucy. Or you have been, until the last couple of days.'

Lucy gave a short laugh. 'Oh, I get it. I'm supposed to be a good girl and resign meekly, not cause you any trouble or embarrassment about the fact you slept with me.'

'No! It's got nothing to do with that.' Nic shook his head emphatically. 'It's nothing to do with you and me. Look, you've been a bit…' He knew he had to choose his words carefully. 'You've been in a difficult situation, with Jack coming back on the scene, and you've been distracted lately. Understandably so. Yesterday, you wrote up the wrong drugs for a couple of patients—luckily the midwife concerned was experienced enough to spot it and double-checked it with me, so no harm was done.'

Her eyes narrowed. 'Are you saying I'm incompetent?'

'No, because you're not. You're a good doctor and I know you can run that ward as well as I can. I said that you'd just reverted to being a doctor like everyone else—one whose handwriting's atrocious and she just hadn't been able to read it properly,' Nic told her. 'But your reports were slapdash yesterday.'

'Is that why you gave me chapter and verse on Tracy Johnson's care?'

He sighed heavily and nodded. 'In normal circumstances, I wouldn't have dreamed of it because you know what to do as well as I do. But these aren't normal circumstances.

And you're not coping, Lucy. Your reports are just as bad today.'

'It's a blip. Temporary. It won't happen again.'

'So what you're saying is, now Nina's been discharged from the ward and you don't have to face Jack again or be reminded of what he did to you, you'll be fine?'

'Yes.'

Nic shook his head. 'I can't risk that, Lucy. It's not fair to the patients. Next time you make a mistake, it could be fatal—and I don't want you throwing your career away over a low-life like Jack Hammond.' Or me, he added silently. 'Take a few days off, get it out of your system. And then I want the Lucy Williams we all know back on the ward, the doctor who should have been a librarian, she's so neat and tidy and organised.'

'I'm fine. I don't need time off,' Lucy insisted. 'Jack's out of my system.'

'Lucy, I heard what you said to Jack just now. You said he'd ruined your life.' Nic's mouth felt as if he'd been eating sawdust. 'That he left you at the altar.'

'So?'

He could see the glimmer of tears in her eyes and hated himself for doing this to her. He wanted to take her in his arms, hold her close and soothe away the pain—but the set look on her face warned him she wouldn't let him touch her. If he tried, she'd only push him away. 'So you're obviously not over him. Or not over what he did to you, anyway.'

One tear started to trickle down her cheek and she scrubbed it away with her hand. 'And you're the man to help me, are you?' she asked nastily.

'I'm here if you want to talk about it, yes,' he said. As her boss? Her friend? His conscience pricked him—as her ex-lover? 'And it'll stay confidential, I promise you that. Anything you tell me is just between you and me.'

'I'm over Jack,' she insisted.

He shook his head. 'It didn't sound like it, just now.'

'And what would you know about it? Mr Dump-them-after-three-dates-if-they-last-that-long!'

He knew he deserved that. But it still stung. 'Lucy, we really need to talk about this.'

'I don't think so. It's none of your business, anyway.'

'Lucy, if your private life affects your work, then it *is* my business,' he said.

'My word, you've got a nerve! You're as bad as Jack!'

'I wouldn't leave my bride standing at the altar.'

'No?'

'No.'

'Then obviously there's something wrong with me,' Lucy said.

He frowned. 'How do you mean?'

'I loved Jack. I thought he loved me. Clearly he didn't.' Pain seared across her face. 'But what I can't work out is what I did wrong. What's so unlovable about me.'

'You're not unlovable.'

'So why didn't he turn up at the church? If he didn't think I was the one for him and wanted to call it off, why didn't he tell me before? Why did he make me wait for him at the church? I never wanted the frills and what have you—I'd have been happy with a quiet little civil wedding. He was the one who wanted the top hat and tails, the vintage car, the champagne and all the trimmings. So why did he make me go through with it when he had no intention of doing it himself? Or am I so slow on the uptake that the only way he could make me realise he didn't want me was to show me in front of all our friends and family?'

'You're not slow on the uptake, Lucy.'

'It was…a nightmare,' she said, her eyes glittering. 'I waited and waited. And all I could think was that he'd been in some terrible accident, that he was hurt or dying or even dead. It never even occurred to me he wouldn't turn up because he didn't want to marry me.

'My sister tried his mobile. It was switched off. And then we realised the best man was there—the best man who was supposed to be with Jack. He didn't know where Jack was either. Nobody knew. I could hear everyone talking, asking what was happening, where Jack was. And then the vicar said he couldn't wait any more, he had another wedding to do and the wedding guests were waiting outside. Everyone was staring as we walked out of the church. The bride, bridesmaids and no bridegroom. No confetti, no organ music, no bells. Trooping out as if it were a funeral, people saying how sorry they were.

'And then I had to face everyone at work. Everyone knew. The grapevine was working overtime. They all knew he'd just stood me up at the altar—and everyone was trying so hard to be kind, nobody actually wanted to talk to me. It's like when someone dies and people cross the road because they don't know what to say and they're too embarrassed to face you. All the whispers and the looks—conversations actually stopped when I came into the room, so I knew they'd been talking about me, speculating about why Jack hadn't wanted me. It went on for weeks. And in the end I couldn't stand it any more. I resigned before I'd even found another job, it was that bad. Luckily there was a position here. And it was far away from London—I wasn't going to have to face Jack again.'

'Don't blame yourself, Lucy. What Jack did was cruel, unfair and spiteful.'

'But *why* did he do it? I mean, I know now he'd met Nina and she was pregnant and he wanted to support her and the baby—at least, he told his mother he did—but why didn't he tell me before? Finding out in front of all our friends and family that he just didn't love me enough to make that commitment—it was just so humiliating. So horrible to have people pitying me and speculating about whether it was my fault or his. Am I so hard to talk to? What's so wrong with me?'

'There's nothing wrong with you, Lucy. And Jack's behaviour was…' Nic searched frantically for the right word but it wouldn't come. 'Vile,' he ended heavily. 'But not all men are like that.'

'Aren't they?' She gave a bitter laugh. 'They are with me. Let's face it, since I slept with you, you've barely spoken to me. Only as much as you had to, at work.'

Guilt balled in Nic's stomach. It was a fair point: he couldn't argue with that. He'd thought he was giving her space, but she thought he'd been avoiding her.

'So it's me, isn't it? The problem's basically…me.'

He shook his head. 'It's not you, Lucy. You're a lovely woman.'

'Oh, spare me the "dear Jane" bit!'

'Look, you're my number two on the ward. We rushed into it without thinking, and now I've had time to step back from the situation a bit. I'm attracted to you, Lucy—more than attracted. You're beautiful and talented and clever and fun to be with. But we have to work together, so we shouldn't get involved.'

'Why didn't you think about that before you touched me?'

'Because I can't think straight when you're around,' he admitted.

She laughed mirthlessly. 'But *I'm* the one who's distracted, according to you.'

'Enough to write up the wrong drugs, yes.'

'OK, so I made a mistake. I'm human. I'm not the first and I won't be the last.'

'You can't afford to make mistakes in our job.'

'I'll double-check in future. You won't be carrying dead weight on the ward.' Lucy folded her arms again. 'But why did you ignore me at work? Why didn't you just tell me you were having second thoughts? Why didn't you ring me at home—or even arrange to meet me someplace in the middle of nowhere so we could talk about it, if you were afraid people were going to gossip about us?'

'I…wanted to give us both some space. Space to decide what we both wanted.'

'What *you* wanted, more like.'

'All right. So tell me—what do you want, Lucy?'

She rubbed one hand across her eyes, dashing away another tear before it fell. 'I don't know now. I thought I knew—but you're not the man I thought you were.' Her mouth twisted. 'No, I stand corrected—you're *exactly* the man I first thought you were. An Italian playboy. Love 'em and leave 'em. What happened between us the other night—it didn't matter a bit to you, did it?'

'Of course it did.'

'So why are you backing off now?'

'I told you. Because we work together and it's too complicated,' Nic said.

'And I'm just supposed to forget that anything happened?' Her eyes darkened with pain. 'I hadn't slept with anybody since Jack. I hadn't even kissed another man until you kissed me at the ball. But you… I let you too close. I thought you liked me. Really, really liked me.'

'I did! I do.'

She continued as if she hadn't heard him. 'But I got burned again. You slept with me and dumped me. Maybe…maybe I'm just useless at sex. Maybe I ought to place a personal ad asking someone to teach me how to do it right,' she said bitterly. 'Someone who won't get involved with me so I won't get hurt this time.'

'That isn't true, Lucy. You're not…' Nic flushed. He was supposed to be giving them both space. Not telling her that sex with her had been mind-blowing and he could hardly keep his hands off her even now. Even now when he was trying to explain that they needed to work through the complications first—the ward, plus the Jack situation. 'Lucy, you're truly lovely. You're everything a man could want.'

'So why did Jack abandon me at the altar? Why did *you* dump me?'

'I can't speak for Jack, and I haven't dumped you.'

'No? When a man completely ignores a woman he's slept with, Nic, it means he's ditched her.'

'I just think…we need a little space, that's all.'

'Which is the nice guy's way of saying, "You're dumped." Give the woman a chance to say it's over first so she feels better about it.'

Had *he* made her this cynical? 'Lucy, I really, really didn't want things to happen like this. I'm sorry.'

'So am I. Because I'll never, ever let anyone get that close to me again. I don't want to go through this again. I don't want to spend all my time wondering what the hell's so wrong with me. Wondering how long it's going to be before the next man in my life decides I'm not what he wants and finish with me without bothering to let me know.' She turned away from him.

'Lucy…' He reached out to her.

She shook him off. 'Leave me alone, Nic. You've done enough. And you're right, I do need some time off. Make up whatever excuses you like for me on the ward. I don't care. Because nothing matters any more.' And before he could say another word, she stood up and walked off.

*   *   *

An hour later, Nic was still brooding in his office, with the door firmly closed. What had he done? He'd wanted Lucy. Wanted her very badly. Badly enough to let it cloud his judgement and make a mammoth mistake for both of them.

But if he'd had the slightest idea that Lucy had been so badly hurt…he'd have let her be. Because Lucy didn't need just a bit of fun, someone to get her out of her shell and let her relax. She needed someone she could rely on. Someone who'd never let her down.—

Could he be the one? Or was he what she thought he was, an Italian playboy who just flitted from one woman to the next?

He'd already let her down. Badly.

What now? Should he go after her and tell her that he'd been stupid, he'd dropped a major clanger but he'd never let her down again? That he'd teach her to trust?

Could anyone teach her to trust? Had she been so badly burned by Jack—and then by what she'd seen as his own betrayal, too—that she'd never be able to trust again?

What a mess. What a horrible, horrible mess.

And he didn't know where to start trying to make things right. *How* to start.

He rested his head in his hands. 'Oh, Lucy. I'm so sorry,' he whispered. 'But I don't know if I'm enough for you. I don't know if I can be the man you want me to be, the man you deserve. I just don't know.'

Lucy took one look at the card that came with the bouquet of hand-tied crimson roses and shoved the whole lot straight in the bin. Did Nic really think that sending her flowers was going to make things all right? He'd done a Jack on her, made it ten times worse by virtually suspending her at work, and he thought roses would smooth things over?

Half an hour later, she fished the flowers out again. It wasn't their fault. And fresh flowers would make the cottage look a bit brighter. The roses looked a little sorry for themselves so she cut a couple of centimetres from the bottom of the stems and placed them in a jug of water. 'Here. A bit of TLC's all you need,' she said.

She removed the bruised petals. There were an even number, she noted. 'He loves me—he loves me *not*,' she said.

And then the tears came. Tears that burned like acid in her soul. Tears that she could only hope would burn away the pain for good. Because she could never, never go through something like this again.

The phone rang and rang and rang. Still no answer. Nic knew for certain that Lucy had an answering-machine. Maybe she'd turned it off for some reason.

But she had to be at home. It was half past ten. He knew Lucy wasn't the pubs-and-clubs type. Hadn't she left the hospital charity ball early even? He drummed his fingers on his knee and tried her pager. It was turned off. Of course—he'd put her on leave for a few days. Why should she leave her pager switched on?

Fear prickled down his spine. She wouldn't have done anything stupid—would she? No. Lucy was too sensible, too level-headed. But on the other hand, she'd been hurt. Badly hurt. She'd lost her judgement at work. And what he'd done had only magnified the Jack situation. Had it been enough to tip her over the edge, make her do something completely out of character?

And if she had...it would be all his fault. He'd never be able to live with himself, knowing he'd done that to her. He had to make sure she was all right. He grabbed his car keys, locked up his flat, drove to her cottage and banged on the front door.

No answer. No sign of a light—but her car was there. So she *had* to be in. He banged on the door again. Still no answer. He was about to smash a window and break in to check for himself when a light flashed on and the door opened.

'What the hell do you think you're doing, Nic?' she demanded.

'I came round to see if you were all right.'

'It's a quarter to eleven,' she pointed out. 'Did it not occur to you that I might be asleep?'

'You haven't answered your phone for two days.'

'There's no law against that.'

Cool, crisp and very much in control. The Lucy he knew and had fallen for. Nic was so relieved that she was OK he actually laughed.

'What's so funny?' she demanded.

'Me. Overreacting. I thought you might have…'

At the look of scorn on her face, he had the grace to flush.

'No, Nic, I haven't done anything stupid. You're not worth it.'

'I was worried about you, though.'

'As you can see, I'm perfectly all right. For someone who's been suspended.'

'You haven't been suspended. You're on leave for personal reasons,' he said.

'Which amounts to the same thing. No doubt I'll hear all the different theories via the grapevine when you finally let me come back to work,' she said drily. 'Now, if you'll excuse me, I *was* asleep.'

'Sorry.' And he noticed that she wasn't wearing anything

under the towelling robe she'd clearly pulled on to answer the door.

Just like the time she'd been wearing *his* bathrobe.

When he'd picked her up and carried her to his bed.

She was still the most beautiful woman he'd ever seen. Even though she was looking as if she wanted to stick knives into him, Nic discovered that the so-called space between them wasn't working in the slightest. He wanted her every bit as badly as he had the first time he'd seen her.

'Foot out of the doorway,' she said. 'Now.'

'Lucy...'

She saw where he was looking and pulled the robe tighter. 'No.'

He rubbed a hand over his jaw. 'I wasn't trying to come onto you just then.' He'd stopped himself. Just in time. 'I really did come round just to check that you were all right.'

'Well, now you know. So you can just go away again, can't you?' And she slammed the door in his face.

It served him right, Nic thought ruefully. Not only had he hurt her, he'd been arrogant enough to think she might have done something stupid because of him. 'Niccolo Alberici, you're a first-class jerk and it's time you grew up,' he said. And he promised himself that he'd leave her alone.

Except he couldn't get Lucy out of his head.

CHAPTER ELEVEN

'IF THAT'S you, Niccolo Alberici, I'm going to say something *extremely* rude,' Lucy muttered, and picked up the phone. 'Yes?' she barked.

'Lucy—thank God you're in. It's Mal. Look, we've got a bit of a problem on River.'

'Sorry, I can't do anything from here. Bleep Nic.'

'He's not answering his bleeper.'

Lucy heard the note of panic in her SHO's voice. 'What's up?'

'I've got a mum in shock. I'm not sure if it's a retained placenta or something worse.'

'Is she bleeding?'

'Yes.'

'Have you done a check for uterine inversion?'

'I'm not really sure what I'm looking for,' he confessed. 'It doesn't happen very often, does it?'

'No. Cord traction on an atonic uterus can do it, or even if the cord's very short, especially when the placenta's right at the top of the fundus,' Lucy said. If it was an inversion, they needed to correct it fast. She knew she wasn't supposed to be at work—Nic hadn't given her the all-clear to return yet—and she'd probably be up for a disciplinary if she went in and he caught her. On the other hand, this was an emergency, Mal was in trouble and since Nic wasn't available she was the only one who could do something. 'OK. Get some fluids into her, get a line in and give her oxygen to deal with the shock. Bleep an anaesthetist and say we want halothane anaesthesia, and get Theatre on standby in case we need to sort it surgically. I'll be with you in ten minutes.'

'Lucy, you're a saviour!' Mal said in relief.

She put the phone down, drove in to Treverro and was on the ward within ten minutes, ready for action.

'Ah, Lucy, you're here, thank God!' Mal said when he saw her. 'The anaesthetist's ready and waiting.'

'I'm going to need your assistance, Mal, if it's what you think it is, because it's a two-person job.'

'Just tell me what you want me to do.'

'First off, the mum's name?'

'Shauna,' he said. 'Shauna Ogilvy.' He led her to the delivery room where Shauna lay on the bed.

'Hello, Mrs Ogilvy—or may I call you Shauna?' At the woman's tired nod, Lucy continued, 'I'm Lucy Williams, senior registrar. Would you mind if I examined you?'

With the patient's permission, Lucy examined her gently, swiftly but thoroughly. As she'd suspected from Mal's hurried briefing, she couldn't feel the fundus—the top of the uterus—when she palpated Shauna's abdomen. 'It's a partial inversion,' she explained to Mal. 'Second degree—the uterine wall's gone through the cervix but it's still inside the vagina. If it's third degree, it comes out of the vagina and if it's fourth degree, it's complete inversion. This really isn't as bad as it could be. Though we need to act now. A tight ring tends to form at the neck of the inversion—and the longer we take to sort this out, the more firmly the cervix contracts and the harder it is to put the uterus back.'

'So what do we do?' Mal asked.

'STAR management. That stands for Shock—which you're already doing—Treat Aggressively and Repair. I want you to get me some cystoscopy tubing, a silastic ventouse cap and two litres of 0.9 per cent warm saline. Using hydrostatic pressure to put the fundus back is a bit old-fashioned and dates from the 1940s, but I prefer it to manipulation because, in theory, stretching the pelvic viscera again could make the mum go into shock.'

And tonight definitely wasn't the time for risky procedures. She wanted tried-and-tested, conservative management. Something that Nic couldn't fault if he happened to come in and catch her here. She moved to stand beside Shauna and held her hand. 'Shauna, what's happened is that your uterus has turned partly inside out, and I need to put it back. I'm going to try to do it manually so we don't have to give you a general anaesthetic and an operation. We're going to give you some drugs to relax the muscles in your uterus and then I'm going to ease it gently back into place. After that, we'll give you something to make it contract properly.'

'Is it going to hurt?'

'You might be a bit sore tomorrow, so we'll give you pain relief,' Lucy said. 'And we'll be keeping a very close eye on you for the next day or so to make sure it doesn't happen again.'

When Ray Edwards had put the anaesthesia in place and Mal had returned with the equipment she'd asked for, Lucy began the procedure, giving Mal step-by-step instructions.

Gently, Lucy held the cap in place and ran the saline through the tubing. Mal followed her instructions and the hydrostatic pressure of the water gradually pushed the uterus back, allowing Lucy to correct the inversion.

'We're there,' she said with a smile. A few deft stitches and she'd repaired the lacerations to the birth canal. 'Now, we need to make the uterus contract to stop the inversion recurring. That means uterine massage, which I'll do now, and uterotonic drugs. What do you think we should give Shauna, Mal?'

'Ergometrine?' he suggested.

'Absolutely right. And very, very close obs.' She winked at him as she performed the massage. 'We'll make a registrar of you yet.' She removed her gloves and went back to Shauna's side. 'We'll let you have a rest before we check you over again, Shauna—you've earned it. But if anything doesn't feel right or you're worried at all, I want you to use your buzzer to call one of the midwives.'

Shauna nodded wearily. 'I'm just so tired.'

'You've just given birth.' Lucy's eyes flicked to the card. 'A big boy, by the looks of things! Nearly four and a half kilos.' She chatted lightly, reassuring Shauna as the anaesthesia was reversed and Mal administered the ergometrine. 'We'll see you later.'

'Thank you, Doctor.'

'I'd better get going,' she said as she and Mal left the room. 'If Nic catches me in here, he'll have my guts for garters.'

'Too right I will,' a cold voice said behind her. 'What are you doing here, Lucy?'

She turned round to face him. 'Got bored, twiddling my thumbs,' she said lightly. 'So I thought I'd pop in and see how everyone was doing.'

'It's my f—' Mal began.

Lucy placed her hand on his arm and made a warning gesture to keep quiet. 'Time for your break, Mal. Catch you later.'

'Shall we go to my office, Lucy?' Nic said.

Lucy followed him in silence, knowing it was an order, not a question.

He closed the door behind them and waited for her to sit down. 'You're supposed to be off until I think you're ready to come back,' he reminded her.

'And you said I wasn't on official suspension,' she countered. 'Strictly speaking, you didn't ban me from the ward. But it's all right, I've got the message. I'm going now.'

'Why were you here, anyway?'

'I told you. Got bored, twiddling my thumbs.' She shrugged. 'Put it down to my...shall we say, faulty judgement?'

And before he could say another word, she walked out.

An hour later, Nic stood outside Lucy's front door with half a dozen bunches of carnations. They should have been roses, really, but the florist was closed and this was the best the supermarket could come up with at this time of night.

Pathetic.

Maybe he should have bought a white flag instead. She might have seen the funny side. Now, she'd think he was trying to schmooze her.

Well, he *was* trying to schmooze her.

Or at least apologise and persuade her to give him a second chance.

He rapped on the door.

'Come in—it's open,' she called.

Nic walked in and nearly fell over a brown-and-white streak that raced towards him, zoomed round his feet and then bounded back over to Lucy and jumped straight into her lap.

'I didn't know you had a puppy.'

'I don't. I'm dog-sitting for my neighbour while she's at the supermarket so he doesn't turn her dining-room table into a coffee-table—aren't I, Bert? Actually, I thought you were her, to come to pick him up.' Lucy rubbed the dog's ears, and the dog leaned back against her, clearly enjoying the attention.

Maybe this was the way to keep her talking to him. Talk about the pup. 'Bert. It's an unusual name for a dog.'

'His kennel name's Treverro Lightning, but Ruth called him Bert. Because of his cheeky little face,' she said, nuzzling the pup, who promptly licked her face.

Nic discovered that it was entirely possible to be jealous of puppies. Especially cute ones like this one.

'I didn't know you were a dog person.'

She shrugged. 'I'd love to have one, but it wouldn't be fair, not with my lifestyle. Changing shifts, never here—the dog'd be on his own too much. Dogs need a family around them. Especially ones like this one.'

'He's a spaniel, isn't he?'

'Yes. One of my stepmothers bred them. I used to...' Her voice trailed off, and he guessed that it was yet another painful memory. One she wasn't going to share with him.

'Why didn't you tell me the full story at work tonight?' Nic asked.

'Nothing to tell.'

'Correcting a uterine inversion isn't "nothing".' His eyes narrowed. 'Mal's told me everything. It seems that Dawn put too much traction on the cord too soon. He knew something was wrong and he needed help. So he called you.'

Lucy shrugged and continued rubbing the pup's ears. 'Don't give him a hard time about it. He was sensible enough to know when he couldn't do it on his own, and you weren't answering your bleeper.'

Nic flushed. 'Flat battery. I didn't realise.' He looked at her. 'I was going to put you on a disciplinary for disobeying my instructions. You knew I'd have to do that if I found out about it, didn't you?'

She nodded.

'But you still came in.'

'The patient has to take priority,' she said simply.

'And you were going to take the flak for it. Even though it wasn't your idea to come in.'

'It *was* my idea, actually. I thought it'd be easier than trying to give Mal instructions over the phone.'

'What am I going to do with you, Lucia *mia*?' he asked.

Lucia *mia*. My Lucy. He'd called her that for a long time, partly teasing. But it was true. He'd thought that it was just for fun, just for now—but it wasn't. It wasn't anything of the sort.

With a shock, Nic realised that Lucy was the woman he'd been looking for all his life. A brave, talented, clever woman who was prepared to put herself on the line for what she believed in. Who put other people first. Who rescued people quietly without making a fuss about it or expecting praise heaped on her. Who'd matched him passion for passion, kiss for kiss, in a way he'd never experienced before.

And he wanted her. He wanted her for always.

But she'd called him 'Mr Dump-them-after-three-dates-if-they-last-that-long'. He'd already let her down. Badly. After she'd been extremely badly burned by her experience with Jack. How was he ever going to persuade her that he was serious about her? That she could trust him?

'I…um…brought you these.' He waved the flowers at her.

'Why?'

She wasn't going to give a millimetre, was she? But he knew he deserved it. 'Sort of another apology. It was the best I could do at this time of night.' He tried for levity. 'Without pinching some from the mums on the ward, that is.'

'No need.'

'Apology accepted?'

She gave him a stony look. 'I didn't say that.'

'Lucy…' Suddenly inspired, he put the flowers on the floor, fished a pen and a white handkerchief out of his pocket and made an impromptu flag. 'Truce?'

He couldn't read the look on her face. He wasn't sure whether she was on the edge of being amused or really, really angry. This wasn't going how he'd planned it—not at all. He shoved the makeshift flag in his pocket and spread his hands. 'I'm sorry, Lucy. I've treated you appallingly. I don't know what to do. I don't know how I can even begin to make it up to you.'

'Forget it.' She made a dismissive gesture. 'We're colleagues. Well, we *were*.'

Nic's heart started to pound. 'What do you mean, were?' Surely she wasn't resigning? Please, no. The idea of her walking out of his life before he'd had a chance to make it up to her, set things right between them…

'I'm off work indefinitely at the moment. A little case of faulty judgement. Being distracted. Putting patients at risk.' She looked up at him. 'Unless, of course, you've changed your mind about that.'

Relief flooded through him. She wasn't resigning. She wanted to come back to work. 'You went for the hydrostatic pressure option. Why?'

'It's easier than lifting the uterus back into the pelvic curve.'

'What if the uterus hadn't gone back?'

'Then I'd have tried manipulation techniques combined with tocolytic drugs, and held the uterus in place until the ligaments had returned to their original state and did the job for me. And if that had failed, I'd have had to go for surgical repair, using the Huntingdon technique. And if *that* had failed, I'd have used the Haultain procedure.' She rubbed the pup's tummy. 'What do you think, Bert? Do you reckon I've passed my viva?'

Nic tried for lightness and gave a soft bark. 'Yes, you have,' he said in a mock-growly voice, as if answering for the pup.

She didn't look the slightest bit amused. His attempt at levity had fallen flatter than a pancake.

'So that's settled. You agree that my judgement's sound. And that I'm not going to put patients at risk.'

'What about Jack?' Nic challenged.

'What about him? I imagine he's back in London by now. Hopefully doing the right thing by Nina. And, before you ask, no, it doesn't bother me. I stopped loving Jack a long time ago. Seeing him again was a shock, I admit. It brought everything back—how bad I felt when he left me. But I'm older and wiser now. I can cope.' She stared at him. 'So can I come back to work?'

Nic nodded.

'Thank you. Have you changed this month's duty roster?'

'No.'

'Then I believe I'm on late tomorrow. I'll see you then.'

She was dismissing him—but he couldn't go yet. Not without asking her… 'Lucy—about us.'

'There is no us.'

'What happened—'

'Was a mistake. A huge mistake,' she cut in. 'You're right. We work together. A relationship between us is completely out of the question. It'd make life far too complicated.' She gave him a tight smile. 'So I'll see you tomorrow. Goodnight, Nic.'

When Nic had closed the door behind him, Lucy stared at the puppy. 'Your eyes are just like his, you know. A mixture of grey and brown. Beautiful eyes. I could fall for you in just the way I fell for him.' Her eyes filled with tears.

'But he let me down, Bert. I thought he cared, *really* cared about me—but I was just another challenge to him. And once he'd conquered me, he lost interest.'

The dog licked her face.

'Three dates and you're out, that's his usual *modus operandi*. I didn't even last one,' she continued. 'And I'm not ever going to let myself get in that sort of situation again. Colleagues, yes; friends, probably not; and lovers, never again.' Her voice broke. 'It'd be so easy to love him, Bert. Look at the way he made that silly flag, just to make me smile. He's like no one else I've ever met. He's got this crazy streak. He makes me laugh. He cooks like an angel. He sings. He…' No. She wasn't going to let herself think about the way he made love. 'But if I let myself get close to him, let myself love him, he's going to break my heart again. And I don't think I'd recover this time.'

She rubbed her face against the pup's soft fur. 'If I give in to the way I feel about him, it'll be wonderful while it lasts—but I know he'll drop me again and he'll hurt me. He won't be able to help himself. He'll always be three-dates-and-you're-out—it's just the way he is. A gorgeous butterfly. So I can't let him get close to me again. I just can't.'

CHAPTER TWELVE

GOING back to work turned out to be easier than Lucy expected. Everyone seemed pleased to see her back but no one said a word about the circumstances leading up to her enforced leave.

Just when she was starting to relax, she hit the first sticky moment.

'Time for a break, Dr Williams.'

She looked up at Nic from her reports and shook her head. 'Sorry. I've got paperwork to double-check.'

'You haven't had a break since you came on duty,' Nic reminded her. 'I need a break, too. Let's go for a coffee at Pat's Place.'

No way. She wasn't going to spend any more time with him than she had to. It was way, way too dangerous. She might start to remember what it had felt like, being in his arms. Touching him. The feel of his mouth against her skin.

No. They were colleagues, nothing more, and she was sticking to that. For ever. 'Thanks for the offer, but I'll pass. I'm cutting my caffeine consumption.'

'Then I'll buy you a mineral water.'

Did he really think they could behave as if the whole mess hadn't happened? As if she hadn't slept with him, as if he hadn't dropped her, as if he didn't know the truth about Jack Hammond and her disastrous attempt at getting married? She lowered her voice. 'Nic—I can't do this. I can't pretend nothing happened and act as if everything's the way it used to be.'

'I'm not asking you to,' he said simply. 'I'm asking my

number two to join me for a quick discussion. Over decent coffee rather than the stewed stuff they drink up here.'

OK, so he wanted to talk about work. But she couldn't handle spending that much time with him. Not on her own. Not yet. Her wall wasn't anywhere near high enough. 'Maybe later.'

He looked at her for a long, long moment. Then finally he nodded. 'As you wish.'

The next week grew even harder, watching Nic chat and flirt with everyone who came onto the ward—everyone from two-year-old toddlers longing to see their new baby brother or sister to great-grandmothers proud to welcome the next generation into the world.

But Lucy noticed that he didn't actually date anyone. Didn't go to lunch with anyone. Didn't go to Pat's Place with anyone.

'The word is, the man's in love,' Mal said.

Lucy flinched inwardly. That was the one thing she couldn't take. The idea of Nic being in love—in love with another woman. Someone who wasn't her.

And had Mal really forgotten her own affair with him that quickly? Given Nic's three-dates-and-you're-out reputation, maybe that wasn't so impossible.

'But apparently she's turned him down.' Mal whistled. 'Can you believe it? I mean, the man makes women swoon from here to John O'Groats and I'd kill to be able to do what he does. But it seems there's one woman in the world who can resist the legendary Alberici charm.'

If only she'd been able to do the same. 'I don't think we should be gossiping about him, Mal,' Lucy said crisply. 'I've got work to do, even if you haven't.'

Nic, in love. Her heart felt as if someone had just asked

it to carry a ten-ton weight. She'd always known she'd have to face the day. She just wished it hadn't come so soon.

Another week passed, this time with Nic switching from the charming flirt to a hard taskmaster who grew more and more short-tempered with his team. Eventually, Rosemary took Lucy to one side. 'Have a word with him, will you?'

'Why me?' Lucy demanded.

'You're his number two. The only one he'll listen to—anyone else, he'll bite our heads off.'

'Come on. This is Nic Alberici we're talking about. The Italian playboy.'

'Who's acting as if someone's just taken all his toys away and he's not a happy bunny. Sort him out, will you?' Rosemary pleaded.

If she protested too hard, people might start to ask why. 'All right. I'll tackle him.' The question was, how to do it without letting him too close to her, without dropping her own barriers.

She waited until the mid-afternoon break, then marched into Nic's office. 'Coffee. Pat's Place. Now.'

'I'm busy. Budgets,' he snapped, not looking at her.

'It wasn't a request.'

That got his attention. His head jerked up. 'What do you mean, it wasn't a request?'

'It means, as your number two, I've drawn the short straw. And I'm definitely not bearding the dinosaur in his den. I want somewhere public where you won't bite my head off—or where someone at least will mop up the blood.'

His eyes narrowed. 'Explain "dinosaur".'

'Tyrannosaurus rex,' she said. 'You know, the stroppy

one who eats people alive for breakfast. Or maybe he just needs a caffeine fix. With one of Pat's muffins.'

Nic stared at her for a long, long moment. She thought that he was going to refuse. And then he sighed and closed his computer file. 'All right.'

'*Very* graciously done, Mr Alberici.'

He gave her a quelling look and they walked in silence to the café. Though this time it wasn't the easy silence they'd always had. This time it was tense to the point where she thought he was going to snap.

'My shout,' she said when they reached the café. Well, the ward's. They'd all given her money and strict instructions to feed him cake. *Lots* of cake. 'Grab a table.'

Nic's eyes widened when he saw the number of muffins she'd bought. 'What's this, one of each?'

'Yep.'

'Lucy, I can't eat all these.'

'There's one from every member of staff.'

'But…' He stared at her, blank incomprehension written over his face.

'You're a pain to work with, Nic. You're grumpy, you don't talk to anyone, you don't smile—the staff are starting to be scared of you, let alone the patients. It's not good for the ward.' She sighed. 'Even cake in industrial quantities clearly isn't going to get you out of this mood. So what's the matter?'

'What's the matter?' He laughed shortly. 'Ah, Lucy. How can you of all people ask me what's the matter?'

'Because I'm not a mind-reader. And neither is anyone else on River.'

'OK. If you must know, I've discovered that a bit of fun, "right here, right now", isn't for me any more.'

'You're talking in riddles.'

'Let me tell you a story,' he said. 'Once upon a time,

there was a prince. A spoiled, selfish prince who did nothing but play all day. And then he met someone special. A princess. She lived in the country next door. He wanted her as his playmate—but she was the serious type and he thought everyone would expect him to build an alliance. And he was sure he'd fail. So he got scared. Backed off. And then he discovered she'd already had a broken alliance, and he felt ashamed of himself for causing her even more pain. He wanted to make it up to her, but she didn't want to play with him any more.'

Lucy met his gaze. 'And?'

'And then something happened. Someone was in trouble in his territory and she sneaked in when he wasn't looking and fixed it. And she wasn't even going to take the credit she was due. He realised what he really felt about her. How very, very special she was. And he spent a long time wondering how he could prove to her that if she had an alliance with him, it would never fail. It would be rock-solid until the end of time. He didn't want to play any more. He didn't want "right here, right now". He wanted more. He wanted always. He wanted her to be his princess, his *principessa*.'

His *principessa*. Nic's old pet name for her. Was he telling her…?

No. She wasn't going to buy into it. Not this time.

'So that's what's wrong with me, Lucy. I've met the woman I want to spend the rest of my life with. And I don't know what to say to her.'

Her judgement had definitely gone again, Lucy thought. Nic didn't want *her* as his princess. Mal was right—Nic had fallen in love with someone who'd knocked him back.

Someone else.

'What do you expect me to say?' she asked, only just managing to keep her voice cool and calm, though she felt as if she were bleeding from every pore.

'I don't know.' He sighed. 'That's one of the problems. We're hardly on speaking terms.'

Lucy stared at her coffee. She was supposed to be doing this for her colleagues' sake. And if he was in love with someone else, it would be better for her anyway. Because it would put him out of her reach and maybe then she'd stop thinking about him, stop wishing for might-have-beens. And, one day, stop loving him.

So why did it still hurt so much?

'Just tell her straight,' she muttered. 'Tell her how you feel.'

'Tell her straight,' Nic mused. 'You think that'd work?'

She didn't meet his gaze. 'It's worth a try.'

'OK.' He paused for long enough to make her look back up at him, and then smiled. 'I love you.'

Lucy's eyes widened. 'You what?'

'I love you, Lucy Williams,' he said simply. Loudly. Loudly enough for every coffee-cup in the café to stop clattering. Loudly enough for everyone to hear him.

The silence was excruciating. Lucy's face flamed. How could he say that? How could he toy with her like this, in front of the whole hospital, after what had already happened between them?

'This isn't the time or the place,' she muttered between clenched teeth.

'Name them and I'll be there.'

'No. No. You're not in love with me, Nic. You're in love with the *idea* of being in love. You were the same at Plymouth.'

'How do you know what I was like in Plymouth?'

'I trained with a doctor on your ward. She was my best friend at med school, actually. And she was always talking about you—how you were a brilliant doctor but the corridors were littered with the broken hearts of the women you'd dated three times and dropped.'

'That's a bit of an exaggeration. I told you before, I'm not a notch-carver. I dated, yes, but everyone knew the rules from the start. It was a bit of fun. And now I'm not in the market for fun any more.'

'That's nothing to do with me.'

'It is. Because you've changed me, Lucy. I love you. No one's even come close to making me feel the way you do. You've eclipsed every memory of every woman I've ever known. And I want you on a forever kind of basis.'

'Maybe I'm not in the market for that.'

'Lucy...I know what happened with Jack devastated you. I know I hurt you, too, and I'm sorry. But it won't happen again.'

'Too right. Because I'm not letting anyone that close to me again,' she said crisply.

'Lucy...you have to take a chance. You'll never find happiness if you refuse to get involved with anyone and cut yourself off from the world.'

'I didn't refuse to get involved with Jack. Or you. And what happened, both times?'

'Don't cut yourself off just because you're scared to try again. If you don't meet happiness halfway, you'll never find it and you'll end up bitter and lonely.'

'There's no guarantee I'll find happiness. And in my experience, looking just leads to heartache.' Lucy pushed her chair back and stood up. 'We're colleagues, Nic. And that's all we're ever going to be. Get used to it. Oh, and don't take it out on the staff any more. Because you'll have found someone else within a week.'

A week in which she avoided him as much as possible. Nic was still mulling over ways to prove himself to her—having rejected skywriting, serenading her or asking her to set him the modern equivalent of the Seven Labours of Hercules—when there was a knock at his office door.

'Nic—have you got a moment?'

Nic looked up from his desk and his heart missed a beat. Had Lucy noticed that her prediction had been wrong and he hadn't even taken a colleague to lunch in the past week, let alone dated or 'found someone else'? Was she about to give him a second chance?

No. Of course not. She'd made it very clear that she'd only talk to him about work. He gave her his best professional smile. 'Sure. What's up?'

'I'm pretty sure I've got a mum-to-be with toxoplasmosis. I wanted to check a couple of things with you.'

'Have you come across a toxoplasmosis case before?' he asked.

'Once, when I was a student. The consultant then said that only about a hundred women a year get tested for it—the rest don't have any symptoms and have no idea there's a problem. It's rare, though probably more common than the official stats show.'

'Yep.' He leaned back in his chair. She was talking to him. About work, yes, but at least she was talking to him. He wasn't going to pass up the chance. 'So what do you know about toxoplasmosis?'

'It's caused by a parasite, *Toxoplasma gondii*—it's usually caught from raw or undercooked meat, unwashed fruit and veg, unpasteurised goat's milk or infected cat faeces. It's easier to prevent it than treat it, which is why we tell expectant mums to wear gloves when gardening or cleaning out litter trays, to cook meat thoroughly and wash fruit and veg,' she recited. 'It's most common in 25- to 30-year-olds and most cases don't show any symptoms. There are around two thousand cases a year in pregnant women in the UK and there's a 45 per cent risk of the baby getting it too. The earlier the mum gets it, the less likely it is to transfer to the foetus but the more severe it can be. It can lead to miscarriage, stillbirth, eye problems or hydrocephalus,' she finished.

'What's the presentation here?'

'She thought she might have glandular fever. She went to her GP with swollen lymph glands in her neck, a headache and general flu-like feelings. He had a hunch it was toxoplasmosis.'

'Could be either—it's not easy to spot.' Nic tapped his fingers on the edge of his desk. 'Did the GP do a blood test?'

Lucy nodded. 'He sent her in with the results. She's got raised IgM antibodies to the parasite—so that means it's a recent infection, not something she caught before pregnancy.'

'OK. First off, we need to find out if the baby's infected. How many weeks gestation is the mum?'

'Thirty.'

'Hmm. It's pretty likely the baby's infected, then—but the good news is that any damage won't be as bad,' he said. 'We'll need to do a scan to see if there's any obvious damage to the foetus. Check with the path lab about the antibodies, because we have to wait four weeks after confirmation of the mum's infection before we can test the foetus. Then we'll need to do a cordocentesis and an amnio, so we can do PCR testing—polymerase chain reaction—on the samples.'

'And in the meantime we give the mum a script for Spiramycine?'

He nodded. 'Four weeks of that, followed by four weeks of sulphadiazine and pyrimethamine—studies show the combination's eight times more effective than the individual drugs on their own, and they also cross the placenta so they'll treat the foetus. Repeat it to the end of the pregnancy. We need to give the mum folinic acid as well, to counteract any reduction in the production of red blood cells. The baby's going to need the same treatment from birth until the end of the first year. We can check his blood for toxoplasmosis from the same sample as the heel-prick test for PKU—' the test for phenylketonuria, a problem with metabolising protein, that was done on all newborns '—and we'll need to keep a check on his eyes for retino-choroiditis.'

'Right. Thanks for your help.'

'You already knew what to do.'

'Just checking. To make sure I'm not being slapdash.'

She left his office before he could respond.

Oh, hell. She was never going to forgive him for that. And it had been partly his fault anyway. He should have seen that she was under too much pressure.

She'd talk to him if she needed him professionally—despite her independent streak, Lucy was sensible enough to know when she needed help—but personally was another matter. He didn't think she'd ever admit it, even to herself.

He'd just have to work harder on melting those barriers around her heart. Find some way of proving to her that she could trust him. That he'd never, ever let her down again. That he loved her more than anything, more than life itself.

Lucy went back to her patient. 'Mrs O'Connor, I'm sorry to have kept you waiting. I just wanted to confirm something with the consultant. Have you heard of toxoplasmosis?'

'It's something you get from cat poo, isn't it?' Danielle O'Connor said.

'Among other things, yes.'

'And that's what I've got?' She frowned. 'But—I don't understand. I haven't got a cat and my husband does the gardening.'

'Have you eaten any meat that's been a little bit pink?'

Danielle shook her head. 'I'm vegetarian.'

'Do you drink goat's milk or eat goat's cheese or yoghurt?'

'Yes. I can't have cow's milk because of my eczema. I get my milk from the farm down the road—but they're ever so good.'

'Unfortunately, it sounds as if that was the most likely source of infection,' Lucy said.

'Is my baby going to be all right?'

'We can do some tests to find out, and there are a lot of things we can do if the baby is affected,' Lucy reassured her. 'I'd like to give you a scan now, if I may. When did you first start feeling ill?'

'Two or three weeks ago.'

'Then it'll be about another week before I can test the baby—we can't do any tests until four weeks after you've been diagnosed. We'll need to take some blood from the baby's cord, and a sample of the fluid from around the baby,' Lucy explained.

She settled Danielle O'Connor back against the couch and performed the ultrasound scan. To her relief, there were no signs of hydrocephalus—water on the brain—or neurological defects on the screen. 'It's looking good from here, but I should warn you now that your baby has a high risk of having an eye problem—though it might not show up until well past his teens. It's called retinochoroiditis. It's when the retina and choroid—that's the light-sensitive surface at the back of the eye—become inflamed and scarred, so there's a slight loss of vision. The good news is that we can give you a course of antibiotics that'll help clear the infection from you—and if the baby doesn't already have it, the drugs will help stop him getting it too.'

'But aren't antibiotics dangerous in pregnancy?' Danielle asked anxiously.

'They can cause problems in early pregnancy, but you don't have to worry as you're thirty weeks,' Lucy said. 'If your baby has it, we'll need to give him the same drugs after the birth until his first birthday, and he'll have very regular check-ups with the eye clinic here. We'll test his blood soon after he's born, but we can use the same sample of blood we use to check newborns for PKU, a condition that affects the way the body uses protein.' She squeezed Danielle's hand. 'We'll do our best by you both, so try not to worry too much. I'll write you a prescription now, so if you don't mind waiting another few minutes we can get the hospital pharmacy to sort out the drugs for you, and I'd like you to come in again in a week's time so we can take the samples from the baby.'

'But I still don't understand how I could have got it. The farm's so *clean*,' Danielle said.

'Goats are more susceptible to the parasite than cows are,' Lucy said. 'And they could have got it anywhere— from their food, or even infected water. It's bad luck, but some people don't even have any symptoms so they don't see us for treatment. At least you've got that on your side.' She squeezed Danielle's hand. 'Start taking your antibiotics this afternoon. If you're worried about anything, give us a ring here, or have a chat with your midwife. And I'll see you next week, OK?'

CHAPTER THIRTEEN

'BLEEP me if you need anything,' Lucy told Rosemary. 'I'm just going to get some fresh air in the park.' To blow the cobwebs away—and hopefully Nic with them. She had to get him out of her head. Somehow.

But before Lucy had even got to the door, there was a blood-curdling scream and a man pushed roughly past her, carrying a wrapped bundle. He ran down the corridor, and as he burst through the doors the alarm went off.

'My baby,' a woman sobbed, staggering through the doorway. 'He's taken my baby!'

'Call Security and look after the mum,' Lucy directed. 'I'll try and catch him up.'

She hurtled through the doors after the man. The display above the lift doors flashed 'G'. It was unlikely that the lift doors had already been open on their floor, and even if they had been, the lift wouldn't have reached the ground floor that quickly. So the man must have taken the stairs. She could hear running feet—had the man headed up or down? She leaned over the stairwell and saw a flash of denim on the stairs above.

Up.

Lucy took the stairs two at a time, using the handrail as a lever to speed her progress, but desperation was clearly driving the man faster. And when he reached the top of the stairs and realised there was nowhere else to go...Lucy swallowed. Please, God, don't let the man do anything stupid. Let him talk to me, give the baby back before someone gets hurt.

But why had he taken the baby in the first place? Who was he? A hundred and one questions flashed through Lucy's mind. And a hundred and one scenarios. If the baby-snatcher went up onto the roof, the baby could suffer from exposure. What about feeding? If the baby was hungry and started wailing for food, would it tip the already unstable baby-snatcher over the edge? Would he jump? Drop the baby?

Be calm. You have to be calm, Lucy told herself. If you confront him and you're panicking, you'll make the whole situation worse. Stay calm, get him talking, and hold his attention until Security or the police can deal with the situation.

Then she heard a door bang and groaned inwardly. It could only mean one thing: the baby-snatcher had gone onto the roof. And it was a bitterly cold November day, the sort with blue skies and bracing winds. Somehow she had to persuade the man to hand the baby back before the infant got too cold. She took a deep breath and climbed the last stairs before the door to the roof.

The man was standing in the furthest corner, close to the edge. Please, no, not a jumper, Lucy prayed.

'Stand back!' he yelled as he saw Lucy.

Lucy lifted both her hands to show she wasn't carrying anything. 'It's OK. I'm not going to hurt you. I just want to talk to you.'

'There's nothing to talk about. Don't you come near me—I've got a knife,' the man warned, 'and I'll use it if I have to.'

Worse and worse. His words sounded slurred. Which meant alcohol, drugs or maybe a medical condition. At this distance, Lucy couldn't tell which. She just had to tread very, very carefully or the baby was going to be in even more danger. And what was the man going to do with the knife? Kill the baby? Himself? Her? 'I promise you, there's no need to use a knife.'

'I don't want you coming near me.'

'I promise I'll stay at a distance. Are you all right?'

'Me?' The man sounded taken aback. 'Why shouldn't I be?'

'Just making conversation,' Lucy said. And if she could keep the man talking long enough, maybe she could persuade him to take the baby back.

'How's the baby?'

'My baby's fine,' the man said, holding the bundle tighter.

'It's cold out here,' Lucy said, 'and newborns lose their body heat very quickly. Can we talk about this inside, where it's warmer—for the baby's sake?'

'Nothing to talk about.' The man half turned away. 'And he's *my* baby.'

'I know. And, sure, you can take your baby for a walk if you want to,' Lucy soothed.

'Don't you talk down to me. You doctors are all the same. If you lot hadn't interfered,' the man burst out, 'she wouldn't have said I couldn't see my baby.'

Lucy thought frantically. Was there a restricted visiting order on any of the patients? She couldn't remember any. 'What's your name?' she asked.

'Why?'

'Just seems funny, talking to someone and not knowing their name, that's all,' she said, hoping that her voice sounded lighter than she felt. 'My name's Lucy. Lucy Williams.'

'Yeah, but you're one of *them*. You won't let me see my baby.'

'There's always a way round a problem,' Lucy said, 'if you talk it through.'

'But *she* won't listen to me. I said I'd change, I said I'd stop drinking, I said I'd go to counselling, do anything she wanted me to. But, no, you lot had been talking to her, you and her parents, brainwashed her into thinking she'd be better off on her own. She said she was getting a new life, one without me, and my baby didn't need me—not now, not ever.'

Lucy waited. Years of training had taught her that if you gave people room to talk, they'd tell you more than if you asked question after question.

'All I wanted was to see my baby. Hold my son.' The man's voice sounded thick with tears. 'She wouldn't even let me see him. I brought her flowers, brought him a teddy, and she threw them back at me. What else could I do?' He cradled his precious bundle against him. 'But now I've got him. She's not going to take him away from me. Not ever.'

'What's going on?' Nic asked Rosemary as he walked back onto the ward and saw several security people. 'What are they doing here?'

'Baby-snatch,' Rosemary said grimly. 'The police are on their way.'

Fear flickered at the base of Nic's spine. 'Where's Lucy?'

'She went after him.'

'Him?' Nic echoed, not understanding.

'The baby-snatcher. Lucy was talking to me at the desk when it happened.'

Nic knew that baby-snatches were very rare, and they were usually done by women. Women who'd maybe just lost their own child and hadn't come to terms with it and were confused enough to think the child they were holding was their own baby. 'So what happened?'

'The baby's father came in and just took him,' Rosemary

said. 'I called Security and Lucy went after him. One of the patients saw them heading upstairs—towards the roof! Even worse, the mum says he's got a knife.'

'A *knife*?' Nic's stomach dived. Lucy was on the roof with a man with a knife?

'She'll be fine. You know Lucy—cool, calm and sensible.'

But what if...? He forced his mind back to concentrate on work. 'How's the mum?'

'Completely distraught. Gemma's with her now, but would you mind looking in on her? Bridget Livesey in room seven.'

'Sure.' Nic didn't dare let himself think of Lucy—or the knife. Was Lucy in danger? Was she a hostage? Was the baby-snatcher threatening to jump? Nic's first instinct was to go up to the roof himself, do whatever he could to save Lucy, but he knew he was needed down here.

Just keep her safe, he prayed. Please, God. Don't let anything happen to her. Don't let anything happen to my Lucy.

In room seven, Bridget was huddled on the bed, rocking to and fro. 'My baby, my baby!' she moaned.

'It's all right, Bridget. We'll get him back for you,' Nic soothed, noting the blue card taped to the baby's empty crib which told him the baby was a boy. 'I don't know if you remember me—I'm Nic Alberici, the consultant. I saw you on my rounds this morning.'

'I don't need you. I just need my baby.'

'I know.' Nic sat down on the bed beside her. 'I'm sorry you're having to go through this right now. But Security are here and they'll get it sorted out.'

'You don't understand,' Bridget sobbed.

'Then tell me,' Nic said gently.

'It's Nigel. I love him, but...oh, I can't live with him.

Not with his drinking. I asked him time and time again to cut down, but then he'd be out with clients and he said he had to drink socially, and he'd be home late, stinking of booze. I told him if he didn't stop, it'd be over between us and I'd bring the baby up on my own. I even left him—I thought it'd bring him to his senses, but he just got blind drunk. He lost his job over it.' Bridget's face twisted in anguish. 'My parents said I'd be better off without him. So I wouldn't let him see the baby—and he came staggering into the ward again today, said he just wanted to give his son a cuddle. I told him to leave and—and—and—he's got a knife!' she howled. 'He took my baby, said I'd never see him again…'

Nic went cold. It was worse than he thought. Not only did Nigel have a knife, he was unstable and drunk. And Lucy was trying to talk him into giving the baby back.

Supposing he stabbed Lucy? Supposing Lucy died before he had the chance to tell her how much he loved her? What was he going to do without Lucy? How could he bear it if she died?

'It's OK. He's upset, he's saying things he doesn't mean,' Nic soothed, trying his best to sound calm even though he was terrified inside and the back of his neck was burning with adrenalin and fear for Lucy. 'He'd never hurt your baby.'

'Not even to get back at me?'

'You said he wanted to see the baby, give his son a cuddle. That doesn't sound like a man who'd set out to hurt a child.'

Bridget gulped. 'He brought Harrison a teddy. I…I threw it back at him, said my baby wasn't having anything from a drunk. If only I hadn't. If only I'd just let him see Harrison, hold him…'

'Hey, don't go blaming yourself. It was a tough situation.

You didn't think he'd do anything like that. He's probably scared himself, too. Our registrar's up there, talking to him. Lucy's brilliant. She'll help calm Nigel down.'

'But what if she can't?'

'Trust me. Lucy can do anything,' Nic said, mentally crossing his fingers. He *hoped* Lucy could calm Nigel down. If she couldn't...it didn't bear thinking about. He checked Bridget's pulse. 'Would you like me to give you something to help you relax?' he asked gently. 'I'm not forcing a sedative on you and I'm not saying you're hysterical—just that you're in a situation that would terrify any mother and it's something that might help you while you're waiting.'

Bridget shook her head. 'I just want my baby. Please. I want my baby,' she moaned.

'I know.' Nic squeezed her hand. 'I'll try and find out what's happening for you.' All he knew right now was that Lucy was on the roof, talking to Nigel Livesey and trying to persuade him to give the baby back. Security was probably holding back, waiting for her signal to move. The only way she could find out more about the situation, things that maybe Nigel hadn't told her, would be if Nic went out on the roof himself. But he needed an excuse, something that wouldn't upset Nigel's already fragile grip. 'When did Harrison last have a feed?' he asked.

'Two hours ago.'

'And you're feeding him yourself?'

Bridget shook her head. 'Bottle. I know I shouldn't. I know you're supposed to do it yourself because it's best for the baby, but I couldn't. I just couldn't.'

'Don't beat yourself up about it,' Nic said. 'Yes, breast milk has all the antibodies and a lot of advantages for both mum and baby, but if you don't want to do it you'll only make feeding time really tough for both of you. Do what suits you both, and don't let anyone bully you into feeling bad about it,' he finished. 'How long since it happened?'

'I don't know. Twenty minutes? An hour? I don't know. I don't know anything any more.' A tear trickled down her face. 'I just want my baby.'

'I'll be back with news as soon as I can,' Nic promised. 'I'll take some formula in case Harrison needs a feed. And between us, Lucy and I will persuade Nigel to give him back. I promise.'

'Nic, you can't. You can't go up there,' Rosemary said when Nic returned to the nurses' station and started sorting out supplies. 'Someone, talk some sense into this man!'

'The baby might need feeding,' Nic insisted.

'And the man's got a knife!' Rosemary pointed out.

'Exactly. Rosemary, Lucy's up there and she doesn't know the full story behind the snatch. She needs help—she needs information. I'm not going to stand by and wait.'

'That's exactly what Security will tell you to do. They're handling it.'

'If the man you loved was up there, would *you* sit back and wait quietly for news?'

'Well—no,' the senior midwife admitted.

'Exactly. And that's why I can't wait and leave Lucy up there on her own.'

'But, Nic, you can't put yourself at risk,' Rosemary said.

'Without Lucy, life isn't going to make any sense. So it really doesn't matter. I'm going up.'

'Nic—'

'We have a day-old baby up there—it's freezing cold, and I don't want him coming back down with hypothermia, frostbite, exposure or dehydration,' Nic said. 'So I'm taking formula, a hat and more blankets. Can someone rustle me up a flask of tea, please?'

'Tea?'

'Tea,' Nic repeated.

Two minutes later, he'd explained his plan to Jeremy, the head of Security, convinced him that he was doing the right thing and was waiting at the door.

'If you're in any trouble, the slightest danger, yell,' Jeremy directed.

Nic pushed through the door.

'Keep back!' Nigel shouted, taking a step backwards, a step nearer the edge.

'What the *hell* are you doing here?' Lucy demanded in an undertone.

'Reinforcements.'

'I don't need reinforcements.'

'Don't argue. You haven't heard the mum's side of things yet,' Nic told her in an equally soft voice. 'Trust me on this.'

Could she trust him?

Professionally, yes. Personally, never in a million years.

And yet this was personal as well as professional. If Nic did the wrong thing now, the consequences could be tragic.

'They need to get together and talk—that's the only way they'll ever be in with a chance of sorting out their problems,' Nic said quietly.

Lucy knew he wasn't just talking about the Liveseys.

'Mr Livesey—can I call you Nigel?' Nic called across to the desperate man in the corner.

Nigel scowled at Nic. 'You've been talking to *her*, haven't you?'

'Your wife told me your name, yes. But I'm not here to judge. My name's Nic Alberici—I'm one of the doctors on the ward.'

'Another busybody,' Nigel sneered.

'Sort of. I've brought something for the baby.'

'What?' He stared at Nic in disbelief.

'The baby. He's hungry,' Nic said. 'Newborns feed little and often. Harrison's last feed was two hours ago. Any second now, he's going to wake up and scream—that's his way of telling you that he wants food. I've brought some milk.' He held up the bottle of formula so Nigel could see it.

'He's *my* baby.'

'I know. So would you like me to show you how to hold him while you feed him?' Nic asked.

'Nic, he's got a *knife*!' Lucy whispered.

'I know that. But he's not going to hurt the baby,' Nic said in an undertone.

'He might hurt *you*.'

'And did you think of that before you came up here?'

'Well—no,' Lucy admitted.

'I came back to the ward and found out that the woman I love was being held at knifepoint! I couldn't just sit back and wait and wring my hands,' Nic whispered back.

'So you just jumped in with both feet?'

'Yes. Just like you did. We're more alike than you think. Just trust me, will you? I'm not going to let anything happen to you. I'm never going to let anything hurt you again.' Nic raised his voice again. 'Nigel—will you let me bring the milk over? And a hat? It's really cold out here, and newborns lose a lot of heat through their head. Harrison really needs a hat so he doesn't get hypothermia.'

'He's *my* baby,' Nigel repeated stubbornly.

'You're his dad. You can give him what he needs,' Nic said. 'Can I bring the stuff over?'

'She can,' Nigel said. 'And any funny business…'

'There won't be any,' Nic promised. 'But I've got a flask of tea for us, too. Can I bring it over?'

'Tea?' Nigel repeated, as if stupefied.

'It's freezing out here. You must be dying for a cup of tea. I was going to bring coffee, but the hospital coffee is so bad you might think I was trying to poison you.' He smiled. 'Sorry, bad joke in the circumstances. I don't mean anything snide by it.'

There was a long, long pause. Then finally Nigel nodded. 'All right.'

'He'll have to put the knife down to feed the baby,' Nic murmured to Lucy. 'When he does, I'll grab it and get rid of it—and then we'll talk him down. Together.'

Once glance at his face showed her that he meant it. He really thought that talking was going to help solve all the problems, smooth things over so Nigel and his wife could make things work.

And he'd come up to the roof, knowing that Nigel had a knife and was unstable—that his own life could be in danger. He'd come here for her sake.

Maybe she'd got him wrong after all. Maybe he wasn't just a gorgeous butterfly. And he certainly wasn't behaving like Jack. In this situation, Jack would have gone straight in the opposite direction, more concerned about saving his own skin. He wouldn't have been worried about her, worried enough to put himself in danger.

'Ready?' Nic asked softly.

'Ready,' she whispered back.

CHAPTER FOURTEEN

TOGETHER, making sure that Nigel could see everything in their hands so he wouldn't panic that they were trying to trick him, Nic and Lucy walked very slowly over towards him.

'Hat first,' Lucy said. 'Are you left-handed or right-handed?'

'Right-handed,' Nigel answered.

'Then you'll need to hold your son with your left arm and support his head on the crook of your elbow, so you can use your right hand,' Lucy directed.

Nigel followed her instructions.

'Now you can put the hat on with your right hand.'

His right hand—the one containing a carving knife—was shaking. 'What about the knife?'

'That's up to you. If you keep hold of it, you might nick the baby's skin while you put the hat on. And scalp wounds bleed very scarily, believe you me. Or you could put the knife down and know your son's perfectly safe in your arms,' Nic said.

Nigel stared at Lucy. She met his gaze without flinching, without moving.

Slowly, he let the knife drop. Lucy smiled and handed him the hat. 'Thanks. Just stretch this over his head.'

As soon as Nigel took the hat, Nic made a lunge, grabbed the knife and flung it over to the ventilation shaft.

'Hey!' Nigel jerked back.

'Nigel, you're going to have to go back downstairs at

some point,' Nic said, 'and it'd be much better for you if the authorities didn't see a knife anywhere on your person.'

'What knife?' Lucy said. 'I didn't see any knife—did you, Nic?'

'No, Lucy, I don't believe I did,' Nic said.

Nigel's eyes narrowed with suspicion. 'Why are you doing this?'

'Because everyone deserves a second chance,' Lucy said. 'I learned that very recently. Sometimes you misjudge people—you think they're going to hurt you when they're really as scared as you are, and the only way things will work out is if you talk things through. If you want to work things out with your wife and your son, you're in a better position to do it if no one can accuse you of holding someone at knifepoint.' She glanced down at the swaddled baby, who was yawning. 'Do you want me to sort out this bottle for you? It looks as if you're going to need it any second now, and it takes a lot of practice to put a teat on a bottle one-handed—Rosemary, our senior midwife, is about the only one I know who can do it.'

'Thanks.' Nigel was still shaking, but both Nic and Lucy knew that the dangerous moment had passed. Nigel was still upset, but no longer close to the edge, close to doing something desperate.

Lucy swiftly took the teat from its sterile wrapping and fixed it onto the bottle of formula. 'It's easier to feed him if you're sitting down. You'd never believe what a weight newborns are,' she said. 'Especially when you're feeding them. Your arm gets really, really tired.'

When Nigel sat down, she handed the bottle of formula to him. 'You just need to keep it tipped up so the teat's always full of milk—that way, you won't get an air bubble,' she said. 'And your son will do the rest of it for you.'

Hesitantly, Nigel put the teat to the baby's mouth. The baby nuzzled, opened his mouth and began to suck.

'This is… It's incredible,' Nigel said, his voice thick with unshed tears. 'My son. My son.'

Nic and Lucy exchanged a glance. 'Shall I be mother?' Nic said, picking up the flask. 'Or shall we all go downstairs and have a cup of tea in the warm, when Harrison's finished?'

'I vote for the warm,' Lucy said. 'How about you, Nigel?'

'I…' He was still gazing in rapture at the baby.

'I reckon that's a second vote for warm,' Lucy decided.

For the first time, Nigel smiled. 'I can't believe you're doing this for me.'

'Like I said, everyone deserves a second chance.' Lucy reached out to touch the baby's cheek. 'Talk it through with Bridget. Maybe you can both compromise, work out what's best for all of you.' She gave Nic a sidelong glance. 'There's a lot to be said for talking.'

'Definitely,' Nic agreed, his eyes warning Lucy that he had a lot to say to her.

The baby finished sucking and fell asleep. 'Do I have to burp him?' Nigel asked.

'Move him so your shoulder's supporting his head, then rub his back,' Lucy said. 'He might bring up a bit of milk—most babies do—so you're better off doing it with a cloth over your shoulder.'

'I didn't think to bring one,' Nic said. 'Shall we go down and get one? All of us?'

The fear was back in Nigel's face. 'What's going to happen to me?'

'I don't know,' Nic said honestly. 'But maybe if you and your wife can talk things through…we'll ask her not to

press charges, and you can work something out between you.'

Nigel was shaking. 'I'll never drink again. I swear it. I
want to be there for my boy—I don't want to be a weekend
dad who hardly ever sees him, never gets to do bathtimes
or be there when he's not well.'

'You need to tell your wife that,' Lucy said gently.

'She told me she loves you, Nigel,' Nic added. 'But she's
downstairs on her own—she's missing her baby, she's
missing you and she needs you both with her. Let's go
down and sort it out.'

'All right.' Still holding the baby close, Nigel stood up
and the three of them made their way across their roof to
the door.

Nic went through the door first. 'Let Nigel carry the baby
back to his mum,' he said softly to Jeremy. 'Let them talk.
And, please, don't take a statement from either of them
until I've had a word with the mum.'

'There are guidelines,' Jeremy reminded him.

'I think this is a situation where we should bend them.
We want to keep this family together,' Nic said. 'Give him
a chance.'

The silence stretched for what seemed like for ever, and
then Jeremy nodded. 'OK. But I'll be keeping a very close
eye on them. Are you coming down now?'

'Not yet,' Nic said. 'I have a little unfinished business.
Five minutes?'

'Five minutes,' Jeremy confirmed.

Nic ducked back out through the door. 'OK, Nigel.
Jeremy—he's our head of Security—is going to go back
down to the ward with you. You and Bridget need a couple
of minutes together—we'll be with you soon.'

'You're not coming now?'

Nic lowered his voice. 'I need a word with Lucy about

something.' Nic smiled wryly. 'You and I aren't so far apart, you know. And if she's in the mood to offer second chances…'

Nigel nodded. 'I get your drift. Good luck, mate—and thanks for what you did for me. For my boy.'

'Pleasure. See you in a bit.'

'Aren't we going down with him?' Lucy asked.

'Not until I've had a word with you.' Nic's mouth tightened. 'Don't you ever, *ever* scare me like that again—taking risks like that!'

'You took one,' she pointed out.

'Yeah. One rule for me, one for you. You do things the *safe* way from now on, do you hear?'

She glared at him. 'Don't you boss me about.'

'We're fighting again. And we need to talk.' His eyes grew dark, intense. 'I love you, Lucy. And when I realised you were up here with an unstable, frightened man with a knife…I couldn't bear it. I couldn't just sit and wait and hope that everything would be all right. I had to do something.'

'You could have pushed him over the edge,' Lucy pointed out.

'He just needed to know that his wife was going to listen to him. That she'd give him a chance to talk things through, work things out.' He paused. 'And that's what I want. To talk things through. Work things out with you—properly.'

Did he mean it? But if he didn't mean it, why had he taken such a risk? Why had he put his own life in danger?

Almost as if he'd read her thoughts—or maybe they were written all over her face—he asked, 'So will you trust me, Lucia *mia*? I know I let you down before, but I won't let you down again. I swear on my life.'

Could she trust him? Her throat dried. 'I—I don't know, Nic.'

'Lucy, I love you. Truly, sincerely...' His voice deepened. 'Passionately. And I want to share the rest of my life with you. I want everything. Dog, babies—marriage.'

'Marriage?' Slowly, she shook her head. 'No. Not after Jack.'

'I'm not Jack,' he reminded her. 'I know I'm rushing this but...I can't hold back. Not now. Not when I was so near to losing you. I need you to know how much I love you, Lucia *mia*. Now and for the rest of our lives. Will you marry me?'

She pursed her lips. 'Aren't you supposed to ask me that somewhere memorable?'

'I am. We're on the skyline of Treverro.'

'We're on the roof of the hospital, Niccolo Alberici,' she pointed out.

'OK. We'll put this conversation on hold,' he said. 'Until our shifts end. Let's go and sort Nigel and Bridget out. And then...we're going somewhere quiet, to talk it through. Just you and I.'

When they got back to the ward, they ignored all the speculative looks. Lucy guessed that Rosemary had said something to Mal and the rest of the team, because no one asked the obvious questions, even though they were clearly bursting with curiosity.

Nigel and Bridget were both in tears, but Bridget had promised to drop charges and Nigel was going to make an appointment with his GP to ask for help with his drink problem. Harrison was happily cuddled on his mother's lap, his father's finger clutched in his tiny hand. 'I think they're in with a chance,' Nic said softly to Lucy. 'I hope we are, too.'

Then it was time to give statements to the police, after which there was a round to do, notes to write up, anxious mums-to-be to reassure…and finally it was the end of their shift.

'Come with me, Lucia *mia*,' Nic said, taking her hand. 'We need to talk.'

'Where are we going?'

'A little place I know.'

As he drove down the narrow roads to the coast, Lucy realised where they were heading. 'Are we going to Pentremain?'

He nodded. 'I discovered it the day I went doing my tourist bit. The day you refused to come with me.'

'It's my favourite place on earth,' Lucy told him.

'Then I think this was meant to be, Lucia *mia*.'

They walked hand in hand to the cliffs overlooking the small bay. The setting sun was a red ball on the horizon and the sky was flushed rose and gold; a single star glittered above.

Nic's grip on her hand tightened. 'Look, the wishing star's out. Remember the song? Starlight, star bright…' He sang the nursery rhyme, his voice soft and low. 'Are you going to make my wish come true, Lucy?' He dropped down on one knee before her. 'I love you, Lucy. I've never felt like this about anyone before. When I heard you were on the roof this afternoon…I was terrified. You were trying to talk a distraught father into giving back the baby he'd snatched—a man who was unstable, probably drunk and had a knife. I thought you were going to die. And I knew my life wouldn't be worth living without you. That I'd lay down my life for you. Will you do me the honour of marrying me—of being my love for the rest of time?'

Lucy was silent for a long, long time. Marriage. It was a risk. A *huge* risk. Her parents were both divorced—several times. Her half-sisters and -brothers were all divorced. She already knew she had lousy judgement in men. Jack had left her at the altar. Nic had rushed her into his bed and dropped her. Could she really take that risk again? Marry him, only to discover later that he'd fallen for someone else and would leave her, the way Jack had? 'I'm sorry. I don't think I can, Nic.'

'I know you've been badly hurt—by me, as well as by Jack Hammond,' he said. 'I understand that. I'd feel the same in your shoes. But what can I do to prove to you that I'll never hurt you again—that I'll never let *anyone* hurt you?'

'I don't know,' Lucy said honestly. 'I don't know if I can trust again.'

'You already have.'

She frowned. 'How do you mean?'

'This afternoon—you had to trust me then. You had to trust me not to send Nigel Livesey over the edge. To help you talk him down. To grab the knife the second he dropped it.'

'That was professional,' she said. 'Part of our job. Of course I trust you professionally.'

Nic shook his head. 'It wasn't just professional. It was *personal*, Lucy. It was about you and me, not just the Liveseys and their baby. You had to trust me to work with you as a team, make sure we all came back safely. We work as a team in our job and it'll be the same in the rest of our lives. You and me. A partnership.' He continued looking up at her. 'I thought I was going to lose you this afternoon. And that's when I discovered that life without you was meaningless. Completely meaningless.'

'That's how you feel now. But how long's it going to last, Nic? You live for the thrill of the chase. What happens afterwards? Three dates and you're out… That's not what I want, Nic.'

'It's not what I want either. I've learned there's a bigger

thrill than that of the chase. Except it's very, very scary. It means taking a risk. It means trusting your judgement.' When she was silent, he continued, 'Remember I told you, a long time ago, that I was looking for the one I wanted to spend the rest of my life with? I found you, Lucy. Then I panicked that maybe I wasn't the right one for you. That's how I knew you were special, because my judgement went completely haywire around you. It scared me. I don't usually rush into things.'

'No?'

'Only with you. Because...' He raked his free hand through his hair. 'I don't know what to say. I don't know how to prove it to you. But I love you, Lucy. You're the one who makes me feel complete. I used to think they were a bit over the top, those songs that claimed the singer would die for his love...but it's true. It's how I feel about you. That's why I came up to the roof this afternoon. So if Nigel was going to hurt anyone, it'd be me, not you.' He tightened his fingers round her. 'This afternoon, you talked about misjudging people, thinking they're going to hurt you when they're as scared as you are. And I'm scared, Lucy. I'm as scared as you are now. The idea of having to spend the rest of my life without you terrifies me. And that's why I'm asking you to marry me. Be my life partner.'

'But marriage...' She shook her head. 'I can't do it, Nic.' Not after she'd been left standing at the church.

'What if you had absolute proof I was there, waiting for you?' Nic asked carefully. 'Would you risk it then?'

'It's not just the getting married bit.' Though that would be bad enough. 'It's afterwards. How do I know you're not going to fall in love with someone else and leave me?'

'How do I know *you're* not going to fall in love with someone else and leave *me*?' he countered. 'It's a risk,

Lucy. But we take risks every day in our job. We make decisions, judgements that could be fatal if we're wrong.'

'That's different. We've both had years of training, years of experience.'

'And the future is something neither of us can predict. So do you face it on your own, or with someone who'll hold your hand all the way, who'll back your judgement?'

'I don't know, Nic.'

'OK. Let's forget about marriage—for the moment.' He stood up again. 'Do you love me?'

Yes. But dared she say it?

'*Ti amo, Lucia mia.* I love you. Heart and soul. If you walk out of my life now, so be it—but no one will ever take your place. And my world won't be in colour any more. It'll be two-dimensional, black and white, a cardboard shell. Mere existence.' He pointed up at the stars. 'And these—their only saving grace will be that somewhere in the world they'll look down on you as well.' He sighed. 'I love you. But if you don't want me, I have to accept that. And I promise I won't make life difficult for you at work. I'll hand in my resignation tomorrow.'

'You'll resign?'

'Why should you have to leave? I'm the one who's causing the problem, not you. So I'm the one who should go.'

'But you've only just been appointed. It'll be terrible for your career, only lasting a few weeks in your first consultant's post. You won't get another chance like that for years and years.'

He shrugged. 'It's just a job. And it's not important to me any more, Lucy. Not without you.'

He'd really give up his career for her? He loved her that much?

And then she realised. Niccolo Alberici might have a silver tongue, he might be charming and a gorgeous butterfly—but he was also selfless, honourable and a man she could trust. She'd had to trust him this afternoon, and he hadn't let her down.

Lucy swallowed. 'Maybe I need someone to—to hold my hand. Teach me to trust.'

'Someone who'd support you and never let you down,' he said. 'I can do that, Lucy. If you'll let me.' He paused. 'What Jack did to you was unforgivable, but you can learn to take a chance again. Show him you're better than he is—that he hasn't made you into the sort of spineless coward he is.'

'By marrying you.'

He shrugged. 'That's one way. But you've already said no.'

'If—and I mean *if*—we get married, I don't want frills.'

He rubbed his jaw. 'We might have a bit of a problem there.'

'How do you mean?'

'You come from a big family, mine's Italian and very extended—so even if we sneak off and get married at Gretna Green with two witnesses from the street, we'd still have to have some kind of party later to celebrate our wedding or they'd all be hurt.'

He had a point. 'You really want to marry me?'

'Yes.'

'Really, really?' she tested.

'Yes.'

When it had come to the crunch, Nic hadn't let her down. And he wouldn't let her down in marriage, the way Jack had. He wouldn't leave her standing at the altar. 'Dr Lucy Alberici. It has a certain ring to it,' she mused. 'So it's all or nothing, is it?'

'All or nothing,' he confirmed.

It was the biggest risk she'd ever have to take. But she

could see the sincerity in Nic's eyes, despite the darkening night, and she knew that she wouldn't be taking the risk on her own. He was going to be with her, every step of the way.

'Then, yes, Nic, I'll take the risk. I'll marry you,' she said softly.

He pulled her into his arms and kissed her. Thoroughly. When he lifted his head again, they were both shaking. 'This wedding,' he said, 'is going to have to be soon.'

Lucy stroked his face. 'I learned something too today, Nic. *Ti amo*. I love you.'

'*Ti amo, Lucia mia*,' he echoed. '*Sempre*. For ever.'

EPILOGUE

ONE month later...

'I'll get it!' Allie called as the doorbell went.

She returned with a single white rose. 'For you, Lucy,' she said, somewhat unnecessarily, and dropped the flower into her sister's lap.

'Don't bend forward,' Susie said, her fingers curled round a strand of Lucy's hair, 'or it'll hurt!'

Lucy opened the card. Nic's flamboyant handwriting informed her, 'I'll see you in one hour. Don't be late.'

'Hah,' she said with a grin, and let her sister continue pinning her hair up.

Thirty minutes later, when Susie was perfectly satisfied with her sister's hair and make-up, Lucy stepped into her dress. The doorbell rang again.

'I'll get it,' Rach said, and returned with a single pink rose.

'Thirty minutes,' the note said.

'This must be costing him a fortune,' Susie pointed out. 'Roses in December. The week before Christmas, no less. And florists deliver on a guaranteed day, not a guaranteed time!'

'Look what he's getting in exchange,' Allie said. 'He's getting our Lucy. Priceless among women.'

'Oh, shut up,' Lucy said affectionately.

'But look at you. I think I'm going to cry,' Rach said. 'You look fabulous.'

'Because my baby sister is an excellent dress designer,'

183

Lucy said. Rach had designed a simple off-the-shoulder raw silk and ivory velvet dress, with a matching velvet stole studded with tiny seed pearls. 'And my middle sister is a dab hand with a make-up brush. And my bossy kid sister helped Nic and me organise everything in record time.' She hugged the three of them. 'I couldn't have done it without you. Any of you. And you all look fabulous.' Rach had made similar dresses and stoles for all of them in crimson, and a fairy dress for her toddler, Lily, in the same material.

'Organising a wedding is a lot more fun than organising a conference,' Allie said modestly. 'I enjoyed it.'

'And who else would I make dresses for, except the one who used to nurse my dollies better when I was a tot?' asked Rach.

'Only the person who let me practise on her and didn't yell when I turned her hair green by mistake,' said Susie. 'The big sister who's always been there for us. And we're here for you.'

A lump rose in Lucy's throat.

'Don't cry—the mascara's not waterproof!' Susie said in horror.

The four of them exchanged watery smiles.

There was a hesitant rap on the door. 'Can I come in?'

'Yes, Mum—she's finished,' Allie called.

Sheena Roberts came into the room, holding her granddaughter Lily's chubby hand, and took a shuddering breath. 'You look fabulous,' she said, her voice cracking. 'Oh, Lucy. You're going to knock them all dead.'

'Not literally, I hope,' Allie said, and they all laughed.

'Nic's going to be so proud of you. So am I. And your dad,' Sheena continued.

'And us,' chorused Allie, Susie and Rach.

'Me!' Lily piped up.

'If you lot don't stop it,' Lucy said, 'I really am going to cry.'

'It's your wedding day. The day you'll remember for the rest of your life—and this time for the right reasons,' Sheena said. 'So put Jack Hammond where he belongs.'

'In the dustbin of history,' Allie said firmly.

When the doorbell rang the next time, it was to announce the arrival of the wedding cars.

'Are you OK, Lucy?' Allie asked when Lily, Rach and Susie had gone ahead with Sheena.

'I think so,' Lucy said. Actually, she wasn't. Her stomach was tied in a complicated knot, the back of her neck felt hot—despite the fact that her nape was bare and there was frost on the ground—and she was sure her hands were shaking. The last time she'd done this, she'd got to the church and waited. And waited. And waited. And then finally had had to accept that Jack wasn't turning up.

But Jack hadn't sent her a rose on the morning of their wedding.

Let alone two.

Make that three, she thought as Allie and her father helped her into the car and the driver handed her another rose—this time, a deep crimson one to match the hand-tied sheaf of roses she carried in contrast with her sisters' sheaves of ivory roses and the teddy Lily was carrying. 'Fifteen minutes,' said the note.

As the car set off, a mobile phone shrilled.

'Good. I was expecting this,' Allie said. 'Perfect timing.'

'Allie, you can't *possibly* work in the middle of your sister's wedding!' Lucy's father said sternly.

'Oh, Roger. As if I'd do that,' Allie teased. 'No, this one's for you, Lucy,' she continued, and handed over the mobile phone.

Lucy went cold. No. It wasn't going to happen all over

again, but this time with the groom letting her know just before she walked up the aisle. Please, no.

But Allie wouldn't be smiling if that were the case. Stop panicking, she told herself. Everything's going to be all right.

Even so, her voice came out as a croak. 'Hello?'

'*Mia principessa.* Did you like your flowers?'

'Yes. Thank you.'

'Ten minutes and you'll be here. The organist's playing Bach, especially for you,' Nic said. 'Can you hear it?'

He'd obviously taken the phone away from his ear for a moment; Lucy could hear the faint sounds of an organ. 'OK. I'm still waiting at the church door. Your mum's just arrived—wow, what a hat. You didn't tell me she was wearing a purple velvet hat! And the girls look fabulous.'

Tears pricked Lucy's eyes. Nic had known how terrified she was of getting married—terrified of it all going wrong at the last minute, of him not turning up and leaving her waiting, just as Jack had done. And this was his way of reassuring her that he was there for her, that he'd always be there for her.

'Oh, and Gina and Sofia are planning to chuck birdfood at us.'

'What?' This was getting surreal, Lucy thought.

'Apparently it's bird-friendly confetti. The vicar's happy because his churchyard doesn't get covered in paper, the birds are happy because they get fed and my big sisters are happy because their aim is lethal. Rach, Susie and Lily have just walked up the path. The teddy's got a dirty face because Lily dropped it. Luckily Uncle Nic has a hankie in his pocket. Hang on, Lily wants a word while I sort out Teddy.'

'Pretty Aunty Lucy,' a babyish voice lisped. 'Princess.'

Lucy gripped her father's hand. 'I'm going to cry.'

'No, you're not,' Roger whispered back. 'You're going to be married to the man you love, to the man who loves you.'

'And I can see the bonnet of your car,' Nic said after retrieving the phone from Lily. 'So I'm going in now— because it's unlucky for me to see you before you walk up the aisle. I love you. And I'm waiting for you, *mia principessa*. I'm waiting for you to make me the happiest man in the world.'

Lucy switched off the phone and handed it to her father, who slid it into his suit pocket and pulled her veil down over her face. And as she took her first steps up the crimson-carpeted aisle to the strains of Purcell's 'Trumpet Voluntary', followed by her sisters and her niece, and saw the love in Nic's face when he turned round to watch her walk to join him at the altar, she knew that he meant it. *I'm waiting for you to make me the happiest man in the world.*

'I will,' she whispered, smiling back at him. 'I will.'

LIVE THE EMOTION

Modern Romance™
...seduction and
passion guaranteed

Tender Romance™
...love affairs that
last a lifetime

Medical Romance™
...medical drama
on the pulse

Historical Romance™
...rich, vivid and
passionate

Sensual Romance™
...sassy, sexy and
seductive

Blaze Romance™
...the temperature's
rising

27 new titles every month.

Live the emotion

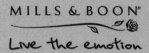

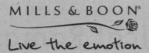

4 FREE

books and a surprise gift!

We would like to take this opportunity to thank you for reading this Mills & Boon® book by offering you the chance to take FOUR more specially selected titles from the Medical Romance™ series absolutely FREE! We're also making this offer to introduce you to the benefits of the Reader Service™—

★ FREE home delivery
★ FREE gifts and competitions
★ FREE monthly Newsletter
★ Exclusive Reader Service discount
★ Books available before they're in the shops

Accepting these FREE books and gift places you under no obligation to buy, you may cancel at any time, even after receiving your free shipment. Simply complete your details below and return the entire page to the address below. *You don't even need a stamp!*

YES! Please send me 4 free Medical Romance books and a surprise gift. I understand that unless you hear from me, I will receive 6 superb new titles every month for just £2.60 each, postage and packing free. I am under no obligation to purchase any books and may cancel my subscription at any time. The free books and gift will be mine to keep in any case.

M3ZEE

Ms/Mrs/Miss/Mr ....Initials................................
BLOCK CAPITALS PLEASE

Surname ....

Address ....

....

....Postcode...............................

Send this whole page to:
UK: FREEPOST CN81, Croydon, CR9 3WZ
EIRE: PO Box 4546, Kilcock, County Kildare (stamp required)